Gunhawk

Jeff Rand, a feared and vengeful gunslinger since his family were murdered, is persuaded by Jim Miller to give up his gunning and join him in peaceful gold-mining. All goes well until one day Jeff returns to camp to find Miller murdered and the gold stolen.

Jeff rides off in a black mood of revenge. But after a saloon fracas, he is forced by gunmen to take part in a bank raid. Then the raiders are ambushed and though Jeff escapes with half the gang, they accuse him of informing and beat him up.

Can Jeff extricate himself? Can he clear his name and can he bring the murderers to justice? Lead must fly before he can find the answers.

Gunhawk

John Long

A Black Horse Western

ROBERT HALE · LONDON

© John Long 1957
First published 1957
This edition published in Great Britain 2009

ISBN 978-0-7090-8787-8

Robert Hale Limited
Clerkenwell House
Clerkenwell Green
London EC1R 0HT

www.halebooks.com

The right of John Long to be identified as
author of this work has been asserted by him
in accordance with the Copyright, Designs and
Patents Act 1988

GLASGOW CITY LIBRARIES	
C0038 99619	
HJ	05-Nov-2009
AF WES	£12.99
	R

Typeset by
Derek Doyle & Associates, Shaw Heath
Printed and bound in Great Britain by
CPI Antony Rowe, Chippenham and Eastbourne

CHAPTER ONE

He was alone. He lowered his gaze from the distant mountains to the nearby pine-clad foothills, then from there to the crimson streaks in the water of the creek wherein he knelt. This was the end. There would be no more saddle-partners for Jeff Rand, and therefore no more griefs. Rand would always ride alone. Cradled in Rand's arms was the bleeding lifeless body of his last friend, old Jim Miller.

'Jim – dead!' he bitterly murmured. 'Seems crazy. Sure he could cuss like pitch, soak up whiskey like he was fire – but a kinder, gentler old-timer never panned gold.'

Blood ran down the corpse; blood dribbled down Rand's chin from where, silencing his grief, he had fiercely bit his lips. How long he knelt there, shocked, and almost sun-drunk by the noonday, he could never tell. A cloud of flies buzzed up from the reeds when, turning stiffly and groggily, he waded to the bankside. He toiled up the slope to a cabin of peeled spruce logs, and, setting his burden on a bunk, once more stood peering lengthily into the dead face, as if hoping for life to reappear.

The air in the cabin was stifling; in fact that cabin was as silent as a desert tomb; and a fat blue-tailed fly, whining round the dead man's head, seemed to enhance the frightening

5

silence. Sinking down upon a goods-box, casting aside a bag of broad-tailed trout which he had been carrying over his arm, Rand hid his face in his hands.

Loneliness as deep as the sky engulfed him. The same thing had happened years ago, miles away, when he was just a kid. At that time his kinfolk had drifted from Texas to Arizona, where desert mining was opening up south of Tucson. There life had been booming real good, same as recently. Then one day his pa sent him hunting a lost burro, which he tracked down right smart for a youngster. How proud he was as he came whooping back into the mining-camp! But all that made the blow more cruel. Singing out triumphantly for Pa and little sister Jenny, he had charged into the shack, and found them brutally murdered.

Then had come this identical profound loneliness, this same resolution to remain lonesome, and this same fierce burning for revenge. After that first tragedy he had become a gloomy and dangerous person, a feared and hated creature of the wilds. But old Jim Miller had changed him, mined a way into his life by simple kindness, and – and here he was robbed and murdered.

'Mebbe if I'd not been so derned mean,' mourned Rand; 'mebbe if I'd quit thinking of spoiling my hands by hard digging, this would never have happened. I shoulda been here helping Jim to wash yesterday's heavy load of dirt, instead of playing hooky, pretending to examine rock upstream. Funny thing, but every sluicing of dirt was leaving bright rich particles at the bottom of Jim's pan, just like it was when Pa died.'

Grief seemed to have turned Rand crazy; for he sat there talking aloud to himself, making appealing gestures to the body, and pausing to examine reproachfully his long and immaculate hands.

'Yeah; Miller's Mine was beginning to pan out big. The realisation of a life-long dream. A big yield for Jim. At last a lucky strike for Jim. Why, only yesterday he talked of moving back to Texas in the Fall. "I'm a-going home, Jeff," he had said. "Home Sweet Home". And then the old fool had started to cry.' Rand chuckled brokenly. 'Poor old fella. Sure enough Jim is home now. By the great Lord Harry! If Jim Miller isn't camped down somewhere in heaven, then – then who the hell is?'

A fiery passion surged through Rand, and his eyes flashed strangely. The blue-tailed fly sped by him and he took a dab at it.

'Death and murder are a coupla different things!' he snarled.

Then the old prospector's last words began to occupy his thoughts.

'Played out, that's me,' Jim had said. 'You ain't to ride after them hoodlums, Jeff. Don't start that life again. The whole hell-raising bunch of them tried to make me talk. They wanted to know about this mine. Guess I'm a mule-headed cuss like your pa used to say. But my luck's come too late, Jeff. I always knowed it would. But you listen here, son. Keep a-digging this claim. I'm a-watching you. Just keep – keep digging – hands clean.'

Slowly Rand raised his head. Jim's voice rang so clearly in his mind that it still seemed a reality. As his moist eyes cleared he abstractedly scanned the raided cabin. The floor was strewn with dried apples, burst flour bags, and shattered boxes of supplies: a whole season's grub-stake lay ruined. In one corner the boards had been ripped up: there was no need for Rand to check Jim Miller's hoard of gold. It was gone. There had been fifty thousand dollars worth of pay-dirt stacked away since they first located this place and filed their claim. Days and nights of hard work lost in a moment; a fortune lost; a partner lost – and now Jeff Rand would always ride alone. This was definitely the end.

While he sat there brooding, with Jim Miller's blood drying on his whipcord breeches and mining boots, the sun had moved round the cabin with surprising quickness. Now it streamed through the small window, brazenly picking out a certain goods-box nailed for a cupboard on the opposite wall. Rand's attention became curiously attached to this cupboard. It seemed to possess some hypnotic power over him, so intensely did he stare at it, while beads of sweat trickled down his nut-brown face. Gradually a more dangerous gleam blazed in his eyes; suddenly he leapt up. He lurched across the room, his tall and skinny body trembling visibly. Having slammed back a table, kicked aside some picks and shovels, he reached that cupboard, jerked open its doors, and dived his hands inside. He clutched at an oil-smeared parcel. But thereat he was stricken motionless by private thought. The moments passed in gnawing uncertainty. His passion died. He bowed his head, giving vent to a soblike groan. Wearily he returned the parcel to its shelf, closed the cupboard doors, and turned away. Choosing a spade he dejectedly strode outside. Rand would bury his partner in the cool and calm of the sunset.

The mountains had become flat silhouettes rimmed by a rosy glow, leaving the foothills half-submerged in mist. A lone bird was piping intermittently somewhere up there. Beside the creek the rhythmic ringing of a spade could be heard. It was a deep down doleful sound, arising from beyond a clump of juniper and mesquite. Presently all went quiet. A tall figure strode into view. He climbed ponderously towards the cabin, only once glancing back at a fresh and ominous mound of earth.

Loneliness, vengeful inspiring loneliness met Rand as he

peered at Miller's empty bunk. Thereon lay the old-timer's simple belongings: a six-shooter, a knife, chaws of tobacco and a watch. But wait! Rand looked again, searched with mounting surprise: the watch was missing. He had presented it to Old Jim on his birthday, and Jim's name was scraped on it. Whoever stole that cheap time-piece had murdered the finest old man on earth.

'The scum! The dirty blazing scum!'

New rage welled in Rand's breast. He strode up and down; he slashed at a whiskey bottle on the window-ledge; the bottle crashed into pieces; he then recognized it as Jim's favourite 'coffin-varnish'. Rand choked between a sob and a curse.

Passion drove him back to that cupboard on the wall. His violent impatience ripped loose the door's hinges. Then, as had previously occurred, something cautioned and restrained the man as his hands closed upon the same stained parcel.

Thereafter Jeff Rand sat on his own bunk before the doorway. He wasn't sleepy; he wasn't hungry; he wasn't even thirsty; he just wasn't nothing. He only wanted to sit, to hide and nurse his injury like a sick animal, same as it had been after burying Pa and little Jenny, years, years, and years ago. Rand began to doze, finding a quaint sympathy in the crickets and bullfrogs chorusing ever louder through the window and open doorway. Peace gradually embraced him, and he felt close to some vague yet grand Presence.

An evasive pearly light was seeping across the sky. An uncommon silence was in command. The dawn was as chill as springwater. Outside the cabin two pack-mules gaped in a kind of astonishment at a saddled and raw-boned horse, which in turn gaped with humorous curiosity through the doorway.

Jeff Rand always rose early. This morning he was haggard and tight-jawed. His mining boots and clothing lay discarded on the floor: he stood dressed in a dark raw-hide riding outfit. The cupboard on the wall was open and empty; and now, on the table, beside a steaming can of coffee and a fry-pan loaded with beans and flapjacks, rested the familiar oil-stained parcel.

Operating between these articles with the calm precision of a craftsman, Rand ate his breakfast and unwrapped a pair of Colt Forty-fives. These well-kept weapons rested snugly in a plain loaded belt. He began to jerk cartridges into the chambers of each gun, his pale and slender fingers working with interesting familiarity. Having then regarded the finished work with some uncertainty, he strapped the belt low round his waist, tied the holsters low upon his thighs, and slammed home each six-shooter.

Standing there in that dawn-filled doorway, leisurely finishing his coffee, Rand looked a changed man – a forbiddingly changed man. Here stood, as even an inexperienced person would have deduced, the figure of a gun-fighter.

CHAPTER TWO

Land of drifting sand, of brightly-painted mountains, of craggy canyons, cacti, scorpions – and heat, parching, cruel heat. A land of strange formations, strange occurrences, and death. This was the Southwest with all its tortures and suffering, and into it came every variety of fortune-seeker. Hardy folk out of the hills, weak folk from the cities; the healthy, the sick, the rich and the poor, the office clerk and the rancher, the good and the bad: all mingled together by the same crazy fever, leaving home and loved-ones far behind, leaving in a moment all they had built by the hard toil of many years, answering that one thrilling war-cry: GOLD!

Jeff Rand was inured to all kinds of hardships and he knew, with that same well-earned knowledge of a ship's navigator, the character of those sea-like desert plains, where already Nature had taken her toll in return for yellow ore. Jeff plodded slowly and steadily through the drifts of hot sand, already regretting his impatience which had so driven him to travel in the sun-hours. Since he had closed down Miller's Mine that morning, he had followed a set of horse tracks which, so he figured, had been left by those riders who had committed the robbery and murder. Before he had left the wooded hills, however, he had noticed that those tracks split up: one set

11

continuing through the beautiful mountain country, and the other descending into the sweltering desert. Following a hunch he therefore found himself entering this broiling hell. Although every mile now weakened his hunch, specially when he viewed his dwindling water supply, he was too stubborn to turn back. Whatever mercy dwelt in his heart, it was being quickly dried up, and replaced by a more flaming vengeance towards the killers.

Through the breathless air and sand finer than snow, Rand plodded from water-mirage to water-mirage. By altered formations of the tracks in the sand he was able to calculate his distance from the riders ahead. The chance of the sand beginning to drift, however, as it did habitually, set him in fear of losing the trail. Yet to urge his mount was too dangerous a thing for him to consider for a moment: the surest way to conquer these plains was by a constant steady pace. His pale blue eyes never ceased to search the hazy distances. Out there, among those acres of mysteriously piled up boulders, lay many a silent warning, lay the whitened bones of men and beasts, the remains of emigrants who had been greedily impatient to reach new gold-fields.

By sundown Rand knew he was gradually overtaking his quarry, who sheltered by day and rode by starlight.

'We'll rest at the first spring,' he murmured, soothing the panting animal beneath him. 'Guess we've done pretty well for the first day.' He licked his parched lips and somewhat anxiously studied his slender hands. 'Yeah; we'll meet 'em come breakfast time, and even scores for our Jim. The dirty bloodlusting scabs!'

The sun was setting in a spectacular glory of scarlet, transforming the sand into a bloody sea, ribbed by shimmering blue shadow-islands. Presently Rand steered away from the trail, craning his neck, looking alertly to the right. The horse grunted. It began to trot quicker. Finally it halted beside a section of stove-pipe stuck upright in a gravel patch. Here the rider dismounted, grinning, inwardly blessing the neighbour-loving prospector who had thus marked and preserved a spring of water from the piling sand. Both wild creatures drank thirstily, ate salted biscuits and rested. Rand wiped down his horse with a wet neckerchief, then softened the leather inside his holsters.

It was not long before loneliness and idleness set him brooding, which brooding inflamed his desire for the show-down. Barely an hour passed by before he was ambling back to the trail. But, to his grim dismay, that trail had completely vanished. Even his own tracks were vanishing as he made them. The sand was on the drift. He could feel no breeze, yet the awful sand was drifting speedily beneath him like water. Bitter frustration filled him. Rand was never a talkative man, yet he could have spoken heated volumes at this moment. His mission of death had failed. His gold was lost forever. Jim's killer must go free. To continue would be surely useless guess-work. He sat motionless, controlling his rising passion, staring with fixed fury into the west. He had to give in. The running desert had won.

Slowly returning to the spring, he became conscious of his exhaustion; moreover the pain in his left foot, which resulted from an old bullet wound, was throbbing sickeningly, and strangely producing fresh pity for his tired mount. There was nothing else to do except camp down for the night. Having gathered together certain juicy weeds round the spring, he tended his horse then brewed coffee. He redressed his foot in an icy wet bandage, then sat with his back to the sleeping animal, whilst he sewed a broken seam in his saddle. Rand's solitary resignation, his silent and independent nature, were characteristic of those hardened desert rats who thrive on

13

sand and sun. He fell asleep, gun in hand.

Time had passed. Jim Miller had now been dead seven days, and Jeff Rand was still alone. Gone was the desert, gone were the enclosing mountains, and all the weary hours of futile searching high and low. Before him there now spread grassy ranges, only interrupted by miniature Grand Canyons and sand-fields which gleamed like ripening corn. Upon the distant horizon a smoky blur marked his destination.

It was late noon when Rand rode into Vulch City, which place was a freak, a one street town where shacks were built from brush and adobe, as well as from barrel sides and bed-blankets. Like similar desert border towns it had begun from a small location of gold. Its first arising was in the form of a row of barrels with planks across them. This had developed into the now largest building, known as Crazy Bill's Saloon.

Rand plodded lazily towards the livery-stable, dismounted by a supreme effort, and led his animal inside, aware that he was watched by a few dreamy and long-faced miners who, obviously poverty-stricken, lounged on the saloon's sun-warped veranda. When Rand returned into the blinding daylight, he gave the whole place a deliberate scrutiny, until his attention fell upon a notice nailed to the opposite shack.

Hash Beans & Roast
No Raw Deals with Sam's Square Meals.
No, sir!
New Arrived: A Whole Bacon!
You Bet!

Rand did not grin. No one should joke about food in this heat-choked and desperate land, specially when a fellow felt like he felt. He wiped the back of his hand across his mouth, wondering just how large was a whole bacon, and just how

14

square were Sam's meals, not to mention his prices. Apparently unaware of the rowdy disturbance which was breaking out in front of that particular eating-house, Rand counted his money as he walked across the street, each spur tinkling at each puff of hot dust. He stopped once to admire an outsize bull-frog squatting in a pool of dampness placed there by a skinny kid who kept poking it with a reed, then looking down the reed at it. Rand might have stayed to see just how the play ended, but he was mighty hungry just then. He climbed on to the raised footwalk. The sound of a fist contacting flesh reached his ears.

'Take that! You're the dirtiest hash-clinger in the whole of creation, and the meanest too!'

Hearing this strange recommending of Sam's square meals, Rand felt a distinct sensation of disappointment. He dropped his few coins back in his pocket and came on, chewing and rolling his tongue. Ahead of him, sprawled on the footwalk, dabbing his blood-smeared face with an apron, was the hash-house owner, Sam. He glared up venomously at his attacker: a short and thick-set young man who wore oddly protruding guns.

'Square meals nothing!' he shouted, disdainfully ripping down the notice, which was quite a masterpiece of lettering on Sam's part. 'Bring out that plateful of filth he served me!' the young fellow commanded one of his companions, thrusting him into the open doorway. 'A coupla jerks of hash should finish him, I reckon, it's poison.'

'You leave my property alone, mister!' groaned Sam.

A loud laugh broke from the small band of hoodlums.

'I'll get even for this, Mister Crocker, I warn you.'

'Sure you will,' replied young Crocker. 'But try this for size first.'

A plate-load of beans was brutally slashed into the injured man's face.

15

'I'll – I'll call the sheriff of Flintstone out to – to these parts. I warn yuh!'

'Try another one,' shouted Crocker, nodding to another of his buddies. 'Make it somethin' a sight more mushy, can't you?'

'Sure, Ted, sure!' A nervous-looking fellow answered.

'Lay off me! Quit it!' howled Sam, his right hand sneaking to his gun.

'Helloa! So you are a gunfighter!' exclaimed Ted Crocker, his eyes seeming to glisten. 'Draw it!' he suddenly hissed, extending and clenching his fingers in anticipation. 'What's the matter? Is it paralysis? Draw your gun, filth!'

Sam noticeably trembled as he lay there, with a mixture of beans and blood running down his shocked face. Gradually his hand crept away from his weapon.

All this sideshow failed to affect Jeff Rand. He seemed to be indifferent to the deadly silence now in command. He sidled through the small gathering of indignant miners, a couple of squaws carrying water-pots on their heads, and a cowering group of open-jawed kids, some peeping over the sidewalk. Rand was just stepping by Sam, gingerly picking his way between slithery pieces of food, when that cocksure and now outraged-looking young man gripped his arm.

'Hey you! I'm Crocker. Where's your manners, stranger?' he purred sinisterly.

Rand felt the tough fingernails cutting into his flesh. He halted, calmly turned his head, and lazily said:

'How-dee!'

'What yuh mean, how-dee? I said where's your manners?'

Rand looked to left and right, as if seeking privacy, then putting his face close to Crocker's, he confidentially said:

'Sh! I sold 'em. Try someplace else, mister.'

Before the astounded fellow fully recovered and under-

16

stood, Rand had viciously cut himself free with a flat-handed stroke and walked on.

A more tensed silence gripped the gathering. Crocker seemed to swell with wrath as he stood there, holding his smarting wrist, glaring at the limping stranger's semi-bent back.

'Rat-face!' he suddenly roared, adopting an aggressive posture, ready to use those protruding guns. 'Stop! Come back here, rat-face!'

The stranger limped onward.

'Why, I'll be a dawg! He is a sham!' Crocker burst into sneering laughter; and his companions chuckled nervously.

It was then Rand halted and lazily turned around.

At last Mister Crocker had a full view of him. The smirk dropped from his face, replaced by deep gravity as he looked up and down that skinny and travel-stained figure of a desert-drifter. He noted the careworn face and the pitying look that fanned his own rage into fiercer flame. Finally his gaze rested on the black Forty-fives. They were tied down. The leather looked soft, well used. Crocker strove to smirk again, yet all he said was:

'I don't like smart-talk.'

Rand nodded understandingly. Everybody could see he sympathised with Crocker's dislike. He turned to go.

'Just a minute!' Crocker's rage was boiling higher.

'Steady on, Ted,' whispered one of the man's buddies. 'He ain't no sham.'

'You shut your jaw! I know a sham when I sees one!' bellowed Crocker, obviously in a state of frustration with his pride. 'So you're a great big awful gunfighter, eh, Mister! Come back, I said. Hey!' He was almost beside himself with rage as Rand again moved away, hurrying. 'Just look at him, fellas! I was right. He moves off like a scared jack-rabbit. He's a no-good sham!'

17

Sure enough Rand hastened out of sight, restlessly rubbing his hands together. In fact his behaviour as he vanished through the eating-house doorway, appeared to be sufficient evidence for the onlookers. Loud guffaws arose from the hoodlums, led in volume by Crocker. Even the poor kids broke out in derisive giggles, and whispered the word 'sham'.

The sham placed himself at a table and bowed his head in his hands. The laughter presently dwindled away and a tinkling of spurs passed down the footwalk. Peaceful silence reigned, only disturbed by a pleasant hissing of steam from behind the counter. Fifteen minutes must have elapsed before the owner entered, wearing a bandage round his pale face.

'How-dee, Mister! Thought you woulda rode on by now.' he mumbled in self-pitying tones. 'Guess you must be real hungry to hang around after what happened. What's your order?'

'One square meal like it said on your board.' replied Jeff, not raising his head.

'Yeah, my board. It took me a whole day to write up that board, rooting out the words from old books and whatnot.' Sam looked mournfully at Jeff. 'You did wise not to tangle with Crocker. Let him have his way, stranger. He's fast with a gun. He's after a big name.'

'Black coffee, please.' said Jeff.

'Coming up,' sang out Sam. 'Naturally we don't stand a chance agin expert devils like Crocker. Confidentially, neighbour, he has this place scared stiffer than corpses. But don't you worry. His likes always get an early coffin.'

'Black coffee, please.' said Jeff.

'Coming up,' sang out Sam; who continued mumbling to himself as he prepared the meal, saying: 'This gent's sure a gloomy cuss. He ain't got no call to be unsociable, cos I took the beating. Like they sez, he's only a sham.'

18

'Black coffee, please.' said Jeff raising his eyes and giving him a piercing look.

Sam jumped guiltily and spilt the coffee. He gaped in astonishment at the dark and emotionless visitor now hunched over a very savoury square meal.

Yes, the food was right good and the charge was fair for a mining town. When Rand left that hash-house he felt a deal better inside and out, having also had a free bath in Sam's tub. He crossed over to the grocery store for some tobacco, called at the livery-stable to settle his account in advance, then counted out his remaining coins. He could buy two drinks, but no more. Sadly he strolled past Crazy Bill's Saloon, a place well patronised to judge by the drone and murmur of voices, and considering the size of Vulch City. Irritably, Rand searched his pockets again. But no; two drinks, then he was broke. He gazed down the parched main street and onward across the plain of brown, shrivelled weeds. He sighed heavily, recalled his attention to nearby, and saw a mongrel noisily lapping from a water-pot, stood beside a sleeping dry-skinned squaw. Rand made his decision. Sullenly he pushed his way through the batwing doors.

The saloon was mercifully cool. Taking his two glasses to a remote table, he sat with his back to the wall. There he rolled tobacco, drank slowly and brooded on his poverty, half-wishing he had remained at Miller's Mine and, as poor Jim advised, kept digging gold.

'Sham!'

Jeff Rand heard his new-earned nickname and recognized the voice of Ted Crocker, although he continued to drink and ruminate, secretly fearing to lose the little peace he was enjoying.

'Stand up, sham! Let everybody see you.'

The noise in the saloon gradually died down. All eyes

turned to Crocker, whose fun-making accents held a distinct note of wickedness.

'This, gents, is a sham. You all know what a sham is, I hope. But has anyone seen the inside of a sham? Well, folks, you're in for a treat. I'm a-going to break this one open, and show you.'

The speaker stood with feet astride in the centre of the ffoor. He was full of pride and confidence, wore a contemptuous sneer, and slid his hands behind his gunbelt.

'Is it an animal or a shell-fish?'asked one of his companions, a thin half-drunk youth who lounged close by at a table, trying to look grim and frightening.

'Let's have no trouble, Mister Crocker. It's time we were riding out,' said another fellow at the table, who smoked a cigar, was dressed in a lawyer-like fashion and had strangely white hair.

'Don't worry, Mister Sturdy. This demonstration ain't going to take long,' growled Crocker. 'Well, sham, I reckon I need an apology. Do I get it, or do I take it?'

At these words the crowd began to laugh nervously.

Three times the young man demanded an apology; each time its importance grew greater with him as he found it harder to get. Three times Rand sipped delicately from his glass, then softly said:

'I apologize, neighbour. I'm real sorry, being a right down awful jackass.'

Somebody in the crowd chuckled. Then everybody chuckled. Pleased by the entertainment he was giving, Ted Crocker also chuckled, but in evil anticipation.

'Hear what he said!' roared some drunken fool at the bar. 'He said he's a – a – a low-down nasty-mannered cuss-pig!'

'Crocker sure understands fellas.' some hidden person yelled. 'His sham wears good-for-nothin' guns, looks hard-

20

skinned, but is mushy underneath, like a tomfool turtle, by hellows-bellows!'

'Thanks Mellons. You're dead right. That's a perfect definition of a sham,' Crocker praised. 'But somehow I figure this one needs a lesson to remember.' he added with a surly growl. 'It's a human insult, his getting rigged up thataway. It's like a soldier wearing a general's coat.'

There came a loud murmur of appreciation at this clever remark.

'Generals work hard and suffer. We just can't have no-account bums insulting their dignity.' shouted Crocker.

'Hear, hear, by damn!' yelled several voices together.

'What's more, I have a special sense of loyalty, and cain't bear to see soft-bellied shams wearing a man's twin guns.'

'You leave me alone.' begged Rand, glaring disappointedly at the crowded doorway, and at all the accusing faces that had somehow found a grievance. 'Just leave me alone, everybody. I said I apologised to you, Crocker,' he mumbled, secretly admiring the man's cunning tongue. 'Just let me go in peace.'

'Let him ride away, Ted. You've won.' said the important looking man with the white hair, who had let his cigar go out as he stared with peculiar intent at Jeff Rand.

Crocker was intoxicated, however, by more than the emotion he had produced in that saloon.

'Fight me, tin-ribs!' he invited Rand, slamming a fist into his palm. 'Let's see how tough you can be.'

Rand declined the offer and took another much-needed drink.

'Then blast you!' bawled Crocker, at last losing his patience, and giving way to his intense hatred. 'Was there ever such a living streak of yolk!' He took a step forward: the crowd pushed back further, its laughter dying. 'All right, Mister Gunslinger, so you won't fight, huh? Then I'm a-coming for your irons.'

Thereat Rand stiffened. His face grew long and sad.

'Not another step with that intention, sonny!' he warned him, gently. 'Go your way. Forget all this. Enjoy life – short enough.'

Ted Crocker looked stupefied. Every man present was visibly shaken, and thrilled by fresh alarm; some guilty ones crouched behind their companions.

Unable to utter another word, such was the angry passion which followed his surprise, Crocker deliberately took another forward step. His face contorted in a killing frenzy. He dived for his weapon. Rapidly he drew it.

But Rand – he did not move; he just sipped from his glass. Yet his right hand was loaded, was squeezing the trigger of a black gun, and stunning the room by a mighty explosion of shots.

Down fell Crocker, writhing in agony: several bullets had torn into his chest. His watch and chain slipped from his waistcoat: the time was four-thirty p.m.

The awful deathly silence that followed seemed to hold everybody spellbound. Rand woefully shook his head, stared bitterly at the remainder of his liquor, then slowly poured it out upon the floorboards. His weapon had been returned to its holster by a secretive, reflex action. The shocked citizens continued to gape at the body. Jeff Rand quietly departed, now really wishing he had not forsaken Miller's Mine.

CHAPTER THREE

Vulch City had looked deserted before the shooting, but now it looked as empty as an ancient tomb. In fact an air of sinister expectation seemed to envelop that skeleton town.

When Rand left Crazy Bill's Saloon, his manner was downright lazy; but as soon as he reached the sidewalk he moved swiftly. He leapt along the creaking boards, reached the livery-stable and dived inside. He began to saddle up, not finding the ostler present. He knew Crocker had dangerous friends: there was only one thing to do, flat-broke as he was and out of provisions, and that was to ride like blasting wind.

Moisture trickled down his face and hands as he worked at the reluctant animal. Flies whined round him, revelling in the stench of sweating horse-flesh and mouldy grain. The heaving and panting of the beasts, the log walls creaking under the sun's heat, suggested that the place might burst into flames at any moment. At last he was ready. He turned with his mount towards the open double-doorway, and halted abruptly. There, standing feet astride in the blinding light, was Crocker's partner, the white haired legal-looking fellow from the saloon – and he calmly levelled two six-guns.

'Leaving us already?'came the gentle inquiry.

Rand relaxed and bowed his head, though his eyes, never

once directly regarding the weapons, fixed themselves on those of the man before him.

'I don't believe even Jeff Rand could beat a drop like this,' went on the amiable stranger. 'No, siree; not even the infamous Rand himself.'

No surprise betrayed itself on Rand's face, although he knew he had never before encountered this person. His first and persistent thought was – how much did the man know of him and the old days?

'The face puzzled me at first,' drawled the other, conversationally. 'But your gunwork clinched my suspicions. I know only four men who draw thataway. Two are dead; one other is a wild fellow named Wyatt Earp who rules Tombstone, and the fourth is . . .'

'The move's yours, Mister Tongue-flapper,' breathed Rand.

'Yes. That's true. No sense in you getting unpleasant, however,' pointed out the mysterious stranger, waving his right gun. 'This is Smily Merrick,' he added; whereat his grinning companion, who had been considerably sobered by the gunfight, stealthily materialised round the doorpost. 'You see, Rand, it's like this. By killing Crocker, who was naturally a fool, you are responsible for us being a man short in our business. Therefore we invite you to join us.'

'What's the business?' Rand bluntly inquired.

'There's grub aplenty, which it seems you need, and the pay's real high.'

'What's the business?' Rand repeated.

'We ain't a-wanting no trouble with you, Mister Rand.' explained Smily Merrick, looking awed by the long and dust-smeared desert-drifter before him. 'Like Mister Sturdy sez, we don't pack no grudge agin you. Crocker got his desserts, fair and square. We just make you a friendly offer.'

'What's the business?' Rand asked once more, looking

bored, almost asleep.

'I'm not in a position to divulge that at the moment,' Sturdy candidly admitted. 'If you need grub and money, then ride with us. The proposition will be set before you when we reach camp. I reckon you owe us something for Ted's death, anyhow. Confidentially speaking, Mister Rand, I have also a personal admiration for you. I need you privately. Well, what's your choice?'

Jeff studied them in a long and unnerving silence. Both were the desperado type, versed in cunning and bloodshed. He could kill the man Sturdy – he knew that by Sturdy's unbalanced gun-grip. Yes; and he might even bring down Smily, who was scared. But the chances of surviving were disappointingly slim. Rand looked cold, without expression on his face as he forcibly restrained himself, feeling that accustomed thrill of gambling with death. He started to think of that food, and the money he needed to continue his search for the gold, and once more concluded with the same question: how much did Mister Sturdy know? Another thing; was there any hope here of a clue to the raid on Jim Miller's Mine?

'What's your decision?' prompted Sturdy, smiling with extraordinary patience.

'Yes, Mister Rand; are you with us?' Smily hoarsely asked.

'Death,' said Rand slowly and impressively, 'seems a mighty hard alternative to following two lousy saddle-bums.'

'Fine,' chuckled Mister Sturdy, spitting out the stub of his cigar. 'Then we have a long day's ride ahead of us. If we leave this stenching pit straightaway, we'll avoid further disturbance and enjoy the cool night hours.'

Mister Sturdy relaxed with a long sigh and hid his guns under his low black coat. Smily Merrick laughed.

Three riders cantered out of town. Upon reaching the high bankside – Vulch City being situated in a dead river course –

the tallest rider looked back, thereat glimpsing the white-aproned saloon keeper angrily leading two bartenders across the street. The bartenders carried a plank between them, whereon rested an ominous shape bound in calico.

This is getting too much like the old days, brooded Rand. Killings and hard riding, so that a fella can't call his will his own no more.

He could remember too clearly how it all began with the avenging of his own murdered kinfolk. That had led to his ending the terrorising career of the Jagger Gang, by beating the notorious Bill Jagger to the draw, a man better remembered as the Prescott Kid. Afterwards had come the life of a hunted beast, wherein either one of the gang or some gun-happy youngster sought to inherit his miserable fame. Sure enough, old Jim Miller had been right. When Jim had given him sanctuary after that cruel foot injury, then offered him a partnership in the mine, he had said:

'Hang up your guns. You're a stranger in this territory, Jeff Rand. Nobody will jump yuh, nobody will give yuh a second look without them guns. You're as safe as Old Man Poverty, and that's me I guess. You and your irons look too close related, and an open challenge for some tomfool upstart. Slap on those guns anywhere, and I warn yuh, Jeff – it's hell-fire.'

The three riders rode steadily onward into the sunset. The sun, as if illuminating a seascape, spread a mighty arrowhead of crimson across a plain of dried brown weed, dotted here and there with grassy islands. Rand's companions maintained a watchful yet amiable silence. Owing to a feeling of being a captive led to some mysterious place of execution, Rand tightened his grip on the reins and rode in the rear.

'Hope you ain't riled with us, Mister Rand,' said Smily.

'No, he's just tired,' observed Mister Sturdy, twisting about in the saddle. 'I think we had better ride close together just in case, though, cos he might take a dislike to us in a dream. Seems his animal don't amount to much neither.'

Jeff said nothing. One hand had instinctively slithered down the weary horse's neck, and was affectionately pinching the quivering flesh. If a quick break became necessary, he knew the other two would be floundering in those accursed sand-drifts far behind him and his gawky desert beast.

As the miles drowsed quietly by Rand kept nodding then jerking up in sudden apprehension. He always found Sturdy, his thick-set body bolt upright in the saddle, watching him piercingly. When their gazes met Rand's jaw stiffened, then Sturdy grinned widely behind his drooping moustache, obviously pleased by something, perhaps by the exchange of Crocker for this new gunfighter.

Eventually Smily Merrick drew his horse close to the gaunt rider, and with a scowl of deep cogitation on his face, at the same time endeavouring to hide his admiration, he said:

' 'Scuse me, Mister Rand, but how come you larned such slick shooting?'

The reply was an awful depth of silence, plainly disconcerting to Smily who shakily added a kind of apology, saying:

'Well, a fella won't get nowhere nohow without asking.'

'Where was yuh headin', Mister?' Rand grunted.

This question flung Smily into a state of embarrassment. He blushed, writhed, cursed because he blushed and writhed, then looked downright stupid.

'Mebbe you was aiming at gunslinging, Mister. If so, you might stake out a claim on boothill,' Rand looked at him with bitter contempt. 'Bridle your tongue, sonny, and you've got control of most things else. Back yonder lies your saddle-buddy, a talkative fella, too cocksure, too tensed for speed. Damn fool kid!' he ended in anger. 'Now he's dead!'

Smily Merrick, mentally noting the professional information,

27

and amazed by striking Rand's hidden emotion for Ted Crocker, drew away his horse in an awe-stricken silence. Smily wanted to think.

It was late in the night when Rand, concerned for his horse, quietly dismounted behind the other two riders who, when they at last noticed his absence, rode back in a sullen frame of mind.

'Thought I said we would ride through the night,' said Sturdy, an authoritative note in his voice.

Rand remained mute, flung down his blanket-roll, unsaddled, and looked for a comfortable spot in the grassy hollow.

'All right, Smily, make camp. We've plenty of time.' Mister Sturdy decided to agree, laughing oddly. 'We'll pool our supplies too. We musn't let this fella starve to death. We might lose a big pay-off.'

'Just one moment,' said Rand, suddenly pausing in his labours. 'What pay-off? What is this here business offer?'

'You'll see, Jeff, you'll see,' Smily quickly assured him.

'I ain't going another step with you, neighbours, till I do see.'

Sturdy and Merrick looked sadly at each other and shook their heads.

'We can't tell you yet, Mister. It concerns rich diggings.' Sturdy nevertheless revealed.

'Real downright sinful rich diggings,' Smily added with excitement.

'We can't stop you from quitting right now, mister, but you're losing a grand position for life,' confided Sturdy.

'A real up-jumping grand position – for life.' Smily chuckled, rubbing his hands together in restless anticipation.

If this concerned gold, mused Rand, obsessed by the robbery and death of his partner, might he not find some unexpected assistance in his search? He conceived a strange

28

hope which he would have found difficult to define at that moment.

'Let's eat, if we can't talk much,' he dryly commented.

A full moon was presently making those wastelands a sight more friendly and mellow. The atmosphere was sweet with the odours of coffee, beans and bacon. A small camp fire flickered across the outstretched forms of three men who, with their heads braced against saddles, breathed heavily in that satisfied air which a good meal provides. Night seemed like a mighty Presence hooded over the vast plain, and occasionally the soothing hush was broken by the distant howling of a coyote.

'Sounds a piece nearer,' remarked Smily.

'Best tie up them hosses close by till daylight,' Rand softly suggested.

'A wise thing, that there,' agreed Smily, jumping up, keen to please him.

'Once heard tell of an old prospector what tied his mules to tree stumps,' Sturdy murmured with yawns, 'and the fools got jittery of the coyotes, hauled up them stumps, and walked off into the night. Come morning the old man went raving mad. Yes, sir, he cussed himself as blue as flame. Then, in those very stump-holes, he saw something shining: it was gold.'

'Lordy me! Luck sure plays funny things,' exclaimed Smily, staking out the animals.

Rand made no comment. But he had raised himself on an elbow and fixed a curiously boring look on the dozing Mister Sturdy.

'I hope these here hosses get to dream-walking,' whispered Smily to himself, returning to his blanket. 'Maybe we'll wake up rich men at dayrise.'

'We needn't worry. Digging ore is hard labour,' Sturdy

pointed out, turning over onto his side. 'Like the boss said: it's a quick and easy pay-off next time for all us boys. It's all fixed up. We'll get rich without digging gold.'

'You bet,' Smily Merrick answered drowsily.

Rand continued to stare piercingly at the figure of Mister Sturdy. No emotion described itself on Rand's face, yet his mind worked excitedly. Was it coincidental that Jim Miller had located gold in exactly the same fashion Sturdy related? Could it be that Fate directed his visit to Vulch City, joined him with these men, and was already drawing his long search to a close? But no; the whole thing was a coincidence; there were thousands of such yarns, of chance discoveries of gold. Every fortune-seeker that scraped the crust of God's earth had his own stock of similar tales, just standing ready to console him when disappointment struck him low. Despite this reasoning, however, Jeff Rand, still determined to follow the faintest trail in a search that might take a lifetime, could not quell his astonishment. Ponderously he asked himself that same question; how much did Mister Sturdy know?

Morning's pallid glow revealed an expanse of grazing land over which the three riders were soon cantering.

'This is old man Keller's spread,' Mister Sturdy informed Rand. 'His ranch lies yonder in Grasshopper Valley. Old Keller used to be the richest cattle-rancher hereabouts, until a few years ago, when sand flooded his prairie. Now the sand's drifting back, howsoever, and Keller looks like becoming cattle king agin, if he lives long.' Sturdy next pointed an arm to the south. 'A coupla day's ride thataway, you will find the desert has started to move in. Herds are dying, crops are shrivelling, ranches sink under hellish gales, and folk are hungered to death's door.'

'Everyone's got his private trouble,' sympathised Rand, appreciating the information. 'A fella has to fight or die.'

'See them mountains straight ahead; those cloud-packs, I mean,' pointed out Smily.

'Yeah, I get them.'

'Well, some say there's gold up there, if only a fella could freight enough water from someplace. But beyond those ranges,' continued Smily, 'lies Flintstone, cattle and mining town, rich as blazes, and worse than Tombstone.'

'Is that where we are headin'?' asked Rand.

Smily and Sturdy laughed in chorus, refused to answer, then went strangely quiet for a long time.

Noonday found them once more in rugged country. The tall prairie grass had grown shorter, yellowed, then rotted to choking dust. Heaps of sand-like earth now lay in wide drifts, where the animals sank to their bellies. Every once in a while Sturdy dismounted, picked up a piece of flint, inspected it, and shoved it in his pocket. There was something really pathetic in this gold-searching craze of his, especially when his pockets grew so heavy he reluctantly emptied them. No one smiled at his behaviour, no matter how comical it was at times. Their journey continued. The land grew worse. A haunting melancholy lay over that once luxuriant prairie, and ragged crows raised a sad lament as they went bug-searching under the withering sun. Suffocating blasts of wind, interrupting an equally stifling stillness, began to rouse spinning dust clouds. Presently dust ran through one's hair and clothing; dust filled eyes and nostrils; nothing escaped that burning, killing dust, forerunner of the flooding desert.

Rand followed his companions across miles of sage-brush flats that day, a kind of shoreline between the sand and the mountains. They rested and ate dried fruits, well pitted with grit, when they entered the foothills. They then proceeded with interesting alertness. Expectation betrayed itself in the actions of Smily and Sturdy. It was sundown when, of a shocking sudden, a shot rang out, splitting the silence like a thunderclap. Two figures appeared in silhouette on a table-top hill.

'Bang away, Smily,' commanded Mister Sturdy.

Smily Merrick slid the Winchester from his saddle-holster. He gave three shots.

Rand, narrowly watching both men who now waved their arms, had an uncanny foreboding of disaster: by tying up with them he was behaving uncommonly rash. He must go on, however; he must follow any flickering hope of regaining his gold and avenging Jim Miller.

'Whiskey, grub, sleep and comforts galore afore long, Mister Rand; you'll see,' promised Merrick, gleefully reloading his Winchester as they rode slowly onward.

'Just leave everything to me,' cautioned Sturdy, gravely patting the dust from his legal-like garb and sliding a well-chewed cigar between his stained teeth. 'I'm the mouthpiece. Remember this, Jeff: keep hands off guns. I'll explain the Vulch City affair sensibly to the boss and Crocker's brother.'

It was these last words, naturally unexpected, which firmly established the grim foreboding conceived by Jeff Rand.

CHAPTER FOUR

The three riders climbed upward and round a monstrous slab of rock. They halted abruptly. Far below them, between towering mountain-sides stretched a rich green gulch. The sudden path of colour, surrounded by the barren landscape, came as a shock to Rand: the place looked unbelievably grand. He could count about two dozen horses way below there, behaving as though they had found Paradise. Against one vertical side of smooth rock, stood three cabins.

Grapevine Gulch, as Mister Sturdy informed Rand, was a hideout more difficult to find than gold quartz. As they descended Rand surveyed the place with mounting curiosity. It was obviously not wide enough for running cattle, nor did those soaring lava-rock walls appear to be gold-bearing. Furthermore it was too remote for use as a health resort. A stronger presentiment of danger gathered in Jeff Rand.

The air grew refreshingly cool as they went lower. With awful grandeur the mountainsides reached over them, forming row upon row of terraces and ramparts, high as heaven itself. Like Smily said: 'One felt as humbled as a no-account bed-bug, riding out between twin knees.' Grapevine Gulch with its two uncannily echoing sides, with its long narrow carpet, possessed a kind of sacred atmosphere, like a cathedral.

'How-dee, boys!' greeted a thin old-timer who, wearing a long grey beard, and with his rearmost end lodged inside half a barrel, sat dozing outside the main cabin.

Rand noticed that the old fellow had a large jug of brew on one side of him, while on the other, cocked and ready, was propped a shining new Winchester.

They dismounted at a spring which spurted and trinkled merrily from the mountain side. As Rand drank thirstily he listened to noises around him: he could hear the clink of dominoes from the nearest cabin, together with greedily chuckling voices and sudden curses of disappointment. To judge by the quality of the curses issuing through that open doorway, the company he was heading into was as tough as the devil, maybe tougher.

'Got a visitor for yuh,' Mister Sturdy announced as he stepped inside.

The result was a silence like death. Rand entered. The blood-red sunset pouring through the window revealed the place. Above him the beams were deep in tobacco smoke; below him the floor was stained with tobacco juice; around him the walls were adorned with crudities from cheap literature; and the air reeked with fried food, whiskey fumes and dirty sweating bodies. Savage eyes watched him intently, studying him from scalp to toe. If hell has any evil stewing places on earth, then this was surely one of them, and Rand was in it.

There were four burly and unshaven fellows at the table, each looking like a private armoury with his guns, bandoliers and knives, either slung round his body, over a chair-back or on the table. Several other less distinct figures sprawled, snoring like sotted beasts, on heaps of supplies and ammunition. The largest man at the head of the table, wrapped one beefy fist round a water-jug, grunted, poured the water over his hairy chest to cool himself, and said: 'Who are you, bony?'

34

'Picked him up at Vulch City, Bruce,' sang out Smily Merrick, leaning on the doorpost and looking nervous. 'He's a rip-snorting gunslick.'

'Is that right, bony,' Big Bruce asked, pugnaciously jutting his chin.

'The boy said it, fatty,' Rand calmly replied.

'Kill it!' the big fellow seemed to explode. A murderous growl rattled in his throat, and he leaped upright with a flaming red face. 'Kill it, Mex! Cut its throat and drag it out o' here. Then let's get on with the game.'

A black-bearded and grinning Mexican ripped out his knife.

'Just one moment.' Mister Sturdy stepped forward, clutching at Mex's wrist, darted a reproachful look at Smily who had stolen his place of spokesman, then addressed himself to the boss.

'Don't refuse the dish afore you try it, Bruce,' he softly advised. 'If it's fighting you want, then just allow me to get out before Rand blasts you all wide open.'

The name hushed everybody. A new expression came into the eyes that scanned the desert-drifter's lanky figure.

'Thought Rand was a big man.' mumbled Bruce, slightly humbled. 'Sure, I've heard tell of him. But see here,' he went on, angry once more, and crashing down the empty water-jug; 'we'll get around to Rand in a minute. Where's the drunken bum you was sent to haul back here? Where's Ted Crocker?'

'Dead!' Smily could not resist interrupting, admiration in his voice. 'Shot stone dead!'

A restless growling and mumbling broke out among the men. But in the corner the drunken snoring continued incessantly.

'Don't talk crazy!' bellowed Bruce. 'Crocker ain't such a slouch with a gun, nor his brother neither.' He directed his

35

narrowed eyes towards Rand. 'What's gone and happened, Sturdy?' he growled. 'Did Ted start talking or something?'

'No. Leastways not about what you're thinking,' Sturdy answered thoughtfully. 'It's like this, there are some gents who don't like being called a sham, least of all Mister Jeff Rand.'

Another deeper hush settled upon them all. The black-bearded Mexican sank back quietly into his chair, slyly sheathing his knife. Even the snoring had ceased now. Big Bruce was nervously wiping his hairy mouth, while self-consciously levelling a sidelong look at the stranger.

'Well!' he bawled, reluctantly trying to sound amiable. 'Seems it's not a bad exchange after all. Mebbe it serves Crocker right, for being a drunken yap-mouth, too big for his pants.'

'But derned fast with a gun,' murmured one awed-looking fellow sprawled over the supplies.

'Why don't you die or something?' snarled Bruce, restlessly massaging his brawny arms.

'It's all right a-talking that way, but what when Jake Crocker hears of this?' asked a hulking individual close to the boss. 'He taught young Ted to shoot; served him like a father; and when he comes in – well, fellas, I think I'll sleep somewhere's else till after the burials.'

'Don't bother, talker,' sneered Bruce; and thereat he crashed his fist into the man's face; it was a vicious, sickening blow from close quarters. 'Best sleeping tonic I knows,' he muttered, licking his bruised fist and grinning at the bleeding and unconscious man still seated there. 'Very well, Mister Rand, everybody's heard something about you, yet it's actions what carry true weight with our outfit. Just understand this, I have no personal liking for gunwork. Any fella can pump lead; it don't take brains. Simply try hard not to kill too many of my boys. Death grieves me at times. That's all, Mister. You're on trial.'

36

'For what?' Rand gave him a sleepy-eyed look.

Big Bruce's head jerked up and he glared malevolently at him, while clenching and unclenching his fists: he never did like a sign of contradiction, it made him think he was losing his authority, to which he clung with anxious greed. Mister Sturdy, observing the clash of wills, and being a born diplomat, judged it expedient to intervene once more. Leaning across the table, he started to whisper confidentially in the big man's thick red ear, which whispering drove away all violent feeling like an extra-marvellous medicine.

Meanwhile the other men toyed with dice and coins, drank from bottles, chewed tobacco, spat with machine-like regularity, and kept directing narrow-eyed looks at Mister Rand. To Rand their behaviour was of persons long confined, quick to quarrel, impatient through much tense waiting, while all the time guarding some tremendous secret with passionate greed and fear. If Rand had conceived foreboding thoughts before, then now, as he waited there under continuous inspection, he had a strong desire to race outside, leap into the saddle, and flee for life's sake. No such inclination was recorded on his face, however. His whole bearing was that of a man who was perfectly at ease, accustomed to riding with all types of men, even anxious about being left all alone, and prepared to shoot down any person who happened to rouse his dislike. He even seemed to be watching hopefully for such persons, for his long white fingers, covertly regarded by all the fellows, kept thrumming his holsters.

'Where's Crocker's brother?' Mister Sturdy presently raised his voice.

'Doing sentry over Rattlesnake Pass,' Bruce replied. 'But don't worry about him. Jake's a sight smarter than Ted was. Jake ain't gun-happy one scrap. Jake will understand how it was. You'll see.'

'Maybe,' mused Mister Sturdy. 'Just maybe. I figger he saw us ride in without his brother. He'll be wondering what went and happened in Vulch City, you bet. Look here, Bruce, you'd best let me explain it to him. You can't afford to lose more men, not at this close stage.'

'Rand, go fix up your hoss,' ordered Bruce, sounding more amiable. 'Show him round the place, Merrick, and wipe that tomfool grin off your gawky face! I'll get Gowl to throw some grub together for you boys. We'll talk bizness, Rand, when you get back. If your second name's poverty, Mister Rand, then mebbe you're due to tie up with Lady Luck. But I ain't making no promises just yet. Remember this fact, I don't stand for no smart-talk from any of my boys, nor any kind of bull-whacking from even you or Symes.'

Symes! That name smote Rand with a force of Bruce's fist, and Bruce watched the effect with evil pleasure. Was Symes here? Was it the same infamous Symes, the same matchless professional gunfighter whose name had spread across the borders? By the great Lord Harry, this outfit was a hunk more dangerous than he'd imagined! Just what kind of play were they making if it attracted Symes? Jeff Rand – knowing once he learned about that play he would never leave this gulch alive – now found his desire to ride brawling with a professional's curiosity to catch at least a glimpse of the notorious Killer Symes.

Ruminating on this, the hope of tracking down Miller's gold, and on Bruce's veiled promise to tie him up with Lady Luck, Jeff followed Smily Merrick outside.

He no sooner disappeared than the men loosened their tongues; the gabbling that broke out was really surprising.

'So that's Rand, the great big man with guns,' sneered Mex. 'Why he's so skinny, so lazy-slow in the head, like a sundrunk pack-mule my father once had. And so you see, fellas, I break him.' He picked up a piece of wood and snapped it across his bulging chest. 'Him, Meester Skinny, thinks he is good. If Jake Crocker no kill, I kill, pronto, you'll see.'

'Sure, we'll see,' sneered Gowl, opening a can of beans on the table. 'And if you don't finish Skinny, mebbe Tom will, and when you all are neat mounds of earth, I'll inspect his innards with this here can-opener. Like hell!'

A sudden bawl of laughter set Mex's eyes flashing madly. He said nothing, but broke another spar across his chest then folded his arms in silent determination.

'Rand shore don't look much, howsoever,' argued Tom, scratching his bristly chin.

'Men like Rand seldom do look much. But take care, because he's got guts,' warned Gowl, slopping the beans on to a plate.

'Aw shucks, quit blowing that trumpet, Gowl. Rand's just a simple kid from the hills someplace. He's sleepy,' yawned one of the snoring addicts in the corner.

'Don't depend on that,' advised Mister Sturdy. 'The tall feller ain't no kid. He has lived like a lone wild creature most of his life. He's poison. I know. I've seen Rand in action more than just once, and when that happens the feller you see simply disappears – the devil takes over. Keep a wise respect for Mister Jeff Rand, boys, and there'll be no bloodshed. He don't strike unless you stand on him – then you're dead.'

'That's nothing.' Tom laughed contemptuously. 'If you think I'm a-going to lick his boots, then you're crazy. I know a few things too, Mister Sturdy. I've travelled around just as much as you, I bet. Last Fall I drifted into Tombstone. There, with my own derned eyes, I saw Whyatt Earp steer clear of Symes.'

'Ah!' a number of voices knowingly exclaimed.

'Symes is fast, faster than blazes and always ready to shoot,'

Gowl declared. 'This outfit was a deal healthier afore it hired Symes.'

'Yeah, having Symes around gives me the warblers,' Mex openly admitted. 'He now is the beeg man, too much for us to handle.'

'Close this pie-jawing, you fools!' Bruce suddenly roared. 'Gunfighting ain't nothing, we have more important things to occupy our minds, remember that. I don't figure to suffer by any more mistakes, and that's why I hired Symes. This time our plan succeeds.'

Everybody fell quiet, watching Gowl nervously slicing up some grisly bacon.

'Where is he now?' Mister Sturdy gently inquired.

'Symes is at Flintstone,' confided Bruce. 'We've been holed up here long enough, waiting for some word from either Clay or Hank. Symes will make those boys skin their eyeballs and work like go-devils.'

'Better than go-devils; you see.' Mex approved, grinning. 'But wait till Meester Symes meets Meester Rand.'

'Why?'

An awkward hush answered that question, because Rand asked it. He was standing in the doorway.

'Hi, there! Roll in, the grub's up,' invited Bruce, oddly kind and respectful. 'Come and get yourself loaded, neighbour. Seems you'll need it.'

Rand conjured up a smile and sauntered forward. At the mention of food, however, a small avalanche had broken out, so to speak. There came a clattering of chairs, a tumbling of supply boxes and an instructive gush of profane language, as every man lunged towards the table.

'Why, you greedy pack of slobbering wolves!' Bruce snarled fiercely, half a loaf clutched in his fist. 'Stand off, or I'll pound you all to flour!'

Mister Sturdy sat down, looking cheerful as he tucked a napkin behind his bow-tie. As usual Rand took his seat with its back to the wall, while Smily Merrick, openly admiring Rand for some hidden reason, stood alongside, using a knife to fish beans from a can.

'Stake yourself a claim with us, and you stay staked,' growled Big Bruce, spraying bread crumbs in Rand's direction.

'Mighty reasonable advice,' agreed Rand. 'Frankly, I'm taking a liking to this outfit. I like the look of the boys, all real amiable, all alert, and ready to jump to it.'

The men had been watching him closely and silently as before, though now, guiltily keeping their hands from their weapons, they nudged each other and chuckled among themselves. Even Mex grinned and winked at Tom.

'Yes, Bruce, as soon as I know the layout I'll make my decision right slick,' continued Jeff, breaking a tough biscuit on the edge of the table. 'Actually, I'm hankering after solid cash to buy me a gold-mine.'

An unrestrained burst of laughter answered his revelation.

'Look here, son,' said Big Bruce in a fatherly kind of manner. 'Our cash will come in such large and solid hunks, as will blast your gold-mine into weekend likker money.' Bruce slammed his fist on the table for emphasis, thereby shocking everybody, as was his habit. 'You won't need any mine when the share-outs come. Hey, Gowl! Drag that infernal door open agin. Let some air into this sour bug-house.'

The Bruce Gang's second impression of Jeff Rand was certainly more favourable. Gowl, wiping a smiling face in his grease-layered apron, obediently flung open the door; Tom rooted out some of his private hoard of tobacco and tossed a chaw to Rand, and Mex served him another helping of bacon. But the bacon was so thin that Smily, nudging Rand, said he

41

could have read the Flintstone Times through it, 'cepting he couldn't read, though he was learning fast. Rand chuckled softly, and Smily felt good to hear him chuckle that way, believing he had struck up a useful friendship with the lone gunfighter.

'Like I was saying, we aim for a big and easy pay-off,' said Bruce. 'Flintstone is the richest of mining towns, and Bulmer's Bank handles thousands of dollars per week as gold-exchange. That kind of money is a great responsibility to the Bulmer boys, Mister Rand, so we figure on being kind to them. We'll relieve 'em of those dollars for nothing, unless they want a hot-lead exchange. Savvy?'

Rand had trained himself to conceal his emotions over a period of many years, yet his underjaw dropped and the biscuit fell from between his fingers as he heard of that intended bank hold-up. Everybody knew that Bulmer's chain of banks were the richest in the territory, and everybody knew that the Flintstone branch was the heaviest guarded. The magnitude of such a robbery would be astounding, and the risk was downright frightening, especially since the recent attempted raids on branches at Maxville and Fairgo City.

'That's some set-up, Bruce,' he murmured. 'A pleasant thought, mind you; but if folk at the bank are already jumpy, I reckon you'll need an army to carry off those dollar bills.'

'Army nothing,' jeered Bruce, looking pompous. 'All I need I now have, and that's a coupla extra boys like Symes and Rand. Sure enough we heard about them other raids. Fact is we made 'em. Twice we were misinformed about the monthly shipment of bills, and lost six men cos of it,' he growled, looking bitterly at the bread he was tearing into with his blackened teeth. 'This time it will be different, by damn!' Viciously he threw the bread out of the window. 'Tell him, Mister Sturdy.' he muttered.

'Bruce sez it will be different now, and he never spoke a truer word,' affirmed Sturdy, lighting his cigar at a flame held out by Tom. 'Already we have Hank Williams installed as a clerk at the bank. Clay's in town too, hired out as sweeper at the saloon opposite, just waiting to bring in Hank's sly go-ahead signal when the shipment rolls in. We judge that shipment to be due any time now, but the two boys were getting jumpy. Clay even packed up his job, but we sent him high-tailing back, under escort of Mister Symes.' Sturdy smiled carelessly at everybody and adeptly shuffled a pack of cards. 'It's easy, Jeff; simply a hunk of huckleberry pie, Jeff. Did I tell yuh that the pickings will be about six hundred thousand dollars.'

'Whew! Rich pickings!' Rand exclaimed, thrusting aside his empty plate. 'Like Bruce sez, it seems I've tied up with Lady Luck.'

Everybody laughed. It reassured and pleased them all to hear the scheme again.

'One thing more, Mister Rand, no gun-blasting without orders,' growled Bruce. 'Keep those guns cold while in this gulch. Ted Crocker was your first and last meat from this outfit. If any fella happens to forget this small point, then Symes will make a neat sluicebox out of him.'

Those final words dwindled in Bruce's throat as he grew aware of the vibrant tension which had gripped the cabin. All eyes stared at the open doorway. Crouching there, sickly-faced and venomous, was Crocker's brother, and he carried a Winchester. It was aimed at Jeff Rand's heart.

'Killed my brother, did yuh?' his voice was an impassioned hiss. 'Sure he was your first and last meat from this gang. Sure Ted was cocky, but he was only a laddybuck.' Jake's voice broke in his gushing hatred. 'Jest a kid, yet you – you murdering, poisonous – why, you ain't fit to breathe fresh air!'

Jake's face contorted in malice. Vengeful satisfaction

suddenly blazed up in his eyes, as he jerked forward the Winchester.

A jolting shot split the silence. It resounded from wall to wall of Grapevine Gulch.

CHAPTER FIVE

The gunshot had come from Rattlesnake Pass. The lookouts were signalling – Symes was coming.

Jake Crocker's reaction was to turn his head, threat he discovered himself peering down the forbidding barrel of a six-gun.

'Drop your Winchester, son!' commanded the old-timer, who had been on guard-duty outside the cabin. 'Somehow I b'lieve your brother found his match in a fair gunfight. Naturally you're grieved some; but if you're bent on making a play for this Rand fella, then do it honest-fashion. There ain't no call for cold-blooded killing, son. Gimme the gun.' He bent closer and lowered his voice. 'Rand's a gun-born natural, Jakey; if you draw it's suicide.'

An angry growling was rising among the men inside. Of a sudden Big Bruce, clutching at a bottle and swinging it up, turned passionately on Crocker.

'Drop it! You're a jackass upstart like your brother Ted,' he snorted in his rage, while liquor coursed down his arm. 'Make your play some time else, mister, and die!'

Still Crocker stood irresolute, his eyes flashing from the menacing bottle to Rand, who idly nibbled biscuit strewn over the table. Jake knew the old man behind him would not shoot, yet he needed time to consider what the situation might be if he surrendered to him. Rand might suddenly whip out a gun and blast him into eternity.

While Jake argued this dreadful problem within himself, a rider had descended into the gulch. On approaching the merrily trinkling spring this rider dismounted, whistling blithely, and covertly digesting the scene visible in the cabin doorway. Beating the dust from his blue flannel shirt, then hitching forward his guns, he came swaggering jauntily to the cabin. Something in his manner, something evasive yet keenly felt by those who watched him, roused a fellow's indignation. It was not merely his conceited smile, nor his boastfully swinging shoulders, nor was it anything visible regarding dress or weapons, it was just like the spirit or soul of the man that communed itself: he was a walking challenge. This was Symes. A light and gay person outwardly, though inwardly his heart and soul were as black as the pit of hell – and the devil himself inspired the swiftness of his hands.

Without respect for age he brutally shouldered aside the old-timer, slammed the Winchester from Crocker's now trembling grip, pressed him back with a clawed hand in his face, then leaned in a leisurely pose against the door-post, still whistling blithely.

Everybody waited for the inevitable, looking from Symes to Rand, and instinctively making a clear passage-way for an exchange of gunfire between the two.

As Symes' gaze settled on Jeff Rand his whistling dwindled away; his lips became a straight line and his nostrils dilated like a beast's. Rand returned the look with blearily squinting half-drunken appearance, as if he had happened upon a new species of reptile he could not make out, although he studied it from tip to tip with natural repugnance as well as interest.

'I don't like you,' whispered Symes, a mirthless grin baring his beautifully white teeth. 'Rand's the name, ain't it?'

Nobody judged it expedient to answer for Rand, and Rand judged it more expedient to hold his tongue. The tension therefore increased. All reverenced the stillness as a long battle of looks was waged.

'Rand ain't it?'

Symes had hooked his thumbs into his broad gunbelt, where the rows of cartridges glittered with evil ostentation. Slowly and stiffly his fingers now outspread themselves. This action was happening without his knowledge, as a serpent-like preparation to strike. Symes had been through all this so often before, that conscious control was no longer necessary.

'Rand!' he sang the word as if it were something delicious on his tongue. 'Mister Jeff Ra-a-and!'

Still no reply came from Rand who studied the speaker with equal intensity, dwelling on the Forty-fives which nestled snugly in long holsters, low-slung, tied down, and slightly tilted. That was the best style, none better, and Rand knew it. Everything about the man roused deep interest in him. He had curly black and greasy hair, a slender figure, just like a woman's, and handsome features, better than many a woman's. But those weapons – they were the most fascinating thing about Symes; and they seemed to possess some hypnotic power, drawing a fellow's attention, as they hung there, from a ridiculously-large gunbelt. If there was any other thing that Rand kept inspecting as much as those six-guns, it was Symes' hands, long and slender and fresh, like his very own. As both men kept watching, just like a couple of animals unexpectedly meeting and weighing each other up, Symes knew he faced a man with courage, and Rand knew he had met a quick gunfighter, but felt he could lick him. The admirable spirit of daring and boldness he sensed flaming in Symes only qualified his dislike when he thought he was beginning to like him.

47

Symes was a killer, seeking to devour, lusting for a fight.

'When I ask questions, I always get answers.' Symes drooled; and now his tapering fingers flexed and reflexed, ready for violence. 'When a fella don't answer, I blast a hole in his stubborn heart. Yuh know why? My name's Symes.'

'How-dee, Mister Chimes.'

'I said Symes.'

'How-dee,' purred Rand, popping a biscuit into his mouth, bulging his jaw and deliberately winking at him.

Symes gaped at him in utter astonishment. He could not believe anybody would have such nerve to do that to his face. At first he became flushed with wrath, then he paled and, surprising everyone, he started to chuckle. A moment later he was roaring with laughter like a son of satan. Rand chuckled, his shoulders shaking. He swallowed the biscuit, and he alone knew with what awful difficulty, then said:

'I like you, Symes, 'cept for one thing. You breathe.'

The laughter died to a ferocious growl in the killer's throat. Every man there shrank further back, but Rand continued to chuckle.

'Well, well, well!' exclaimed Symes, striving to recover his composure, forcing himself to grin then laugh again. 'You and me have a lot in common, Mister Rand. Yeah, seems this outfit is beginning to look and act tough at long last. It's derned interesting, though noways healthy for a peace-loving fella like myself.'

The men breathed with relief, nodded and smiled mean-ingly to each other and cast puzzled looks at Jeff Rand. They had found a new respect for him, yet Rand knew they distrusted him no less. In a really charming manner Symes swaggered inside, whereat one of the burly fellows at the table became nervously quick to vacate a seat for him. Symes sat down and thudded his feet on the table, insultingly close to Rand.

'You've got guts, mister,' he praised, pouring drinks for them.

'Shore, mister; and you've got big feet,' Rand pleasantly informed him, slowly yet firmly pushing them aside.

'You're all right, Jeff, you don't get scared,' mused Symes, looking thoughtful and voluntarily withdrawing his limbs. 'Mebbe I could use a man like you for some private business someday. Yeah, mebbe I will.'

'What happened at Flintstone?' asked Big Bruce, who had been trying to get the question in for a long time.

'What happened here?' Symes countered his question. 'What was the gun-show about as I came in? Do you want me to straighten out these hell-raising Crocker boys for yuh?'

'Aw, that weren't nothing. Rand plugged Jake's brother in Vulch City. Everything's fine now, though,' Bruce explained, trying to keep his voice level and bold, yet his eyes had strayed to Symes' guns.

'Go on, go on. Tell the rest of it,' urged Symes, looking highly pleased and eager, and pouring more drinks for himself and Rand.

The Boss proceeded to relate the gunfight, helped in detail by Mister Sturdy who had been champing excitedly on his cigar throughout this time, and who at the present moment was maintaining a sly watch over Jake Crocker. It was clear that fear of Symes duelled with Crocker's hatred for Rand. He could not speak. He just stood back against the wall, and stared and stared at Jeff Rand, his eyes ablaze from interior fire.

'Seems I shoulda went to Vulch City not Flintstone.' Symes ruefully shook his head. 'Guess I miss stacks of good raw entertainment thataway, pleasing other folk.'

'Never mind that. What about the shipment o' dollars?' Bruce began to shout with impressive authority. 'When is it due? Did you scare any sense into Hank Williams? Do yuh reckon he'll stay on as clerk till we bust in? Well, Symes, well?'

'Have you finished croaking, fat-belly?' snarled Symes. 'You've got quite a gunful o' questions, ain't yuh?'

Big Bruce rolled restlessly in his chair and viciously bit at a quid of tobacco. He glared around him at his staring men, then fired a stream of tobacco-juice through the cabin window. Symes was playing with him, and he knew it, and what was worse half the outfit was present, all keenly watching him lose his dignity as leader. It was right down maddening. These skinny gunmen, Bruce reflected, were all branded alike; all big-headed; all tough and talkative as long as they carried six-guns. Bruce entertained a secret loathing of gunplay, and he longed to give Mister Symes, but now especially Rand whose calm manners somehow infuriated him the most, a sound and lasting lesson in fist-play. Another stream of powerful tobacco juice sailed through the window. Bruce was certainly feeling his weakening authority in the presence of these professional gunslingers.

'All right, all right. Evidently you went on a fool's errand, Symes. Mebbe you didn't even see Hank Williams.' Bruce tried again, with an effort to look unconcerned.

'Cool off, fat-belly!' sneered Symes. 'Naturally I saw Hank. He was preparing to slug the bossy president of the bank when I rode into town. Hank said he didn't like his job in the express office, but after a little pow-wow he even started to hanker after being president himself.'

'What you mean? You ain't gone and killed him have yuh?' Bruce glared anxiously into the killer's face.

'Clay has settled down agin at the saloon,' Symes continued, ignoring the question, 'and he too has got real ambitious now. He likes sweeping floors. He said he would like to sweep saloons all over the derned country, till he was dead, for me.'

Bruce began to understand; he looked around him, a sickly grin on his face, which grin reflected in the faces of the other men.

'Thought sending you would do the trick,' he said, conceitedly. 'How about the shipment, though. When's it due?'

'That shipment o' dollars arrives at Bulmer's Bank, Flintstone, somewheres over a week from the present day,' Symes stated, with sighing endurance. 'Hank sez he'll signal exact time to Clay. Clay sez he'll ride hell-fire for here. I say I'm dead tired, hungry, and fed up with your dictating attitude, fleshy-guts. So throw some grub out here and leave me in peace.'

The low murmuring that the news brought from the men nevertheless pleased Symes, who smirked contemptuously at them. The shipment was definitely arriving at Flintstone; each monthly shipment was always greater than the last, so fast was the mining town prospering. Only one thing tempered the satisfaction of this knowledge, and that was another spell of waiting, wherein war would be waged between a growing anticipation and fear.

During the last few moments Jake Crocker had been filling his pockets from the cracker barrel and wrapping two bottles in a blanket. He was now prepared to leave; but, turning in the doorway, he directed a malicious look across the cabin, and said:

'Mister Rand! You ain't getting my brother's share o' dollars. You ain't a-taking his place. You murdered him, say what you like. And I'm a-going to kill yuh!'

A dreadful quiet was created by those words. The quiet was shockingly broken by a boisterous guffaw. That was Symes.

'Ted Crocker had a fair chance to beat me, neighbour,' Rand softly addressed Jake. 'You get the same chance.'

51

'He smells, Jeff! He's a skunk-cabbage!' Symes insulted Crocker whose eyes bulged wider. 'Go on, kid, pack a gun for Mister Rand, and we'll see you pack a coffin. Hopes I'm a bystander to this play, Jeff, I want to see how you work on small fry.'

Rand glanced sharply at Symes, whose laughter sank low. Another battle of looks waged between them, to be broken when Crocker brutally slammed the door behind him, shuddering every plank in the place.

'Try to calm the kid down for us, Mister Sturdy,' sighed Big Bruce, pouring himself a mugful of liquor. 'We'll be needing every fella on the job what's coming up.

'No powers of talk are going to alter Jake much,' murmured Mister Sturdy, shoving a pack of cards back into his vest pocket and preparing to leave. 'I'll do my best, of course, but not tonight.'

'Look here, Rand, you'd better use the small bunk-house with Mister Sturdy,' said Bruce; then, suddenly crashing his fist on the table, he leaned forward in a towering rage. 'There'll be no more gun-slamming, Rand! Do you hear?'

'Naturally. Reckon your voice carried a coupla generations back,' Rand dryly remarked. 'I aim to kill no fella, if no fella aims to kill me.'

Bruce felt he had already borne enough impudence from Symes, and therefore Rand's remark inflamed him, seemed to choke him, and make him look tremendously hot for a human being. Had he to sit there and be over-ruled by every gun-packing saddle-bum that rode into the place? Why, before long he would be doing the chores for the whole confounded outfit. Impulsively Bruce crashed back his chair, drew himself to his full height, which candidly amazed Jeff Rand, and glowered down at everybody.

'I'll crush yuh to a bloody pulp!' he roared, his voice

deafening in that confined space. 'I'm running this camp. You will keep your guns cold, Rand. Fust sign o' violence and, by the bowels of hell, fella, I'll pound yuh to gravel. That's final.'

He shook a great meaty fist in front of Rand's face, and Rand flushed and tensed. Rand felt Symes and Sturdy and all of them eagerly watching him. Sure enough he was scared, yes, and scared of Big Bruce too, yet he raged inside like a furious fire. But he dare not touch his guns just then. There was nothing else to do but surrender to the humiliation, unless he desired to fist-fight Bruce, which would ruin him for life anyhow, hands and all. Gradually by a supreme effort Rand controlled his wrath.

'Don't nobody ever sleep around here?' he drawled, with a pretence of stifling a yawn.

'Just follow me, Jeff,' Mister Sturdy replied quickly in relieved tones. 'Yeah, just follow me; you too, Smily. Good night, boys!'

'Rand will get a chance to prove himself soon enough; you'll see,' Bruce called after them forebodingly, his face plainly recording disappointment.

'He sure will,' added Symes, releasing another of his noisy guffaws.

Jeff halted halfway to the door. Were they deliberately goading him, perhaps testing him? Slowly he turned and stared mournfully at Symes.

'Our future should be real interesting,' he muttered, ominously.

'I'll make it interesting, and exciting,' Symes promised him with wicked kindness. 'Good night, Mister Rand.'

Slowly and thoughtfully Rand passed outside. He felt downright uneasy.

Moonlight streamed through a certain cabin window, revealing phantom forms of sleepers to Jeff Rand, who could not sleep. Apart from himself, the cabin was occupied by Sturdy, Merrick and Gowl the cook. Mister Sturdy had use of the only bunk in the place; the remainder were rolled in blankets on the floor, using saddle-bags for pillows. Rand's boots and guns lay close beside him, one of each to right and left, as caution had taught him. His thoughts, ponderously battling with his great weariness, concerned a variety of things. But mostly he wondered just how fast Symes was with a gun. Another thing, did Symes rule the gang? Certainly Bruce did not appear clever enough for that position, and for the planning needed to hold up Bulmer's Bank. But never mind; none of it mattered; Rand would quietly ride away at daybreak. It was none of his business. Still, how fast with a sixshooter was Mister Symes?

Stealthily the moonlight crept across the floor. Jeff, watching its yellow richness, thought of gold. He then wondered despairingly of ever finding Miller's yellow ore; next he mused on those peaceful days at Miller's Mine. That was the only time he had really felt content, truly at ease, for years. Now old Jim was gone. Witty old Jim; good old Jim; he could see him now, grinning mischievously round his corncob pipe.

The moonlight had faded; that infernal bull-frog had quit raising mischief at the spring out yonder, and the sizzling of crickets had dwindled at last into nothing. Deep sleep engulfed Rand.

CHAPTER SIX

Rand did not ride from Grapevine gulch next morning. He postponed his break with the Bruce Gang until next day, and then the next: a vague suspicion, a hunch which could not be defined, held him in captivity. Rand could not sacrifice his only slim lead to finding Miller's killer and the gold.

During this time, as the raid on Flintstone bank drew nearer, he became affected by the mounting excitement amongst the men. To hear them talk imparted anxious thrills of expectation, made him curious as to how the play might pan out in the end, but also roused guilty feelings on his own part. Rand had done many a shady thing in his life, just like everybody, but he had never ridden with a gang and raided a bank. What was more he was not inclined to that kind of liveli-hood, and he was a-going to get himself a few hundred miles away afore he was hauled into such big business. Anyhow, the boys now began to squabble as regular as a starving wolf pack in the gathering tension, creating more immediate dangers.

Fearing trouble, knowing they mistrusted him and grudged him a share in the profits, Rand began to indulge in exploring rides among those rugged mountains. Sometimes Smily Merrick strung along with him, pleased to believe he was Rand's saddle-buddy. Sure enough Smily was cheerful company to a lonesome fellow, and Jeff had a secret liking for Smily. But he allowed it to become no more than just a liking, because Smily's light-hearted nature kept roping in memories of poor Jim, which all re-established his resolution of no more partnerships for grief's sake. Occasionally Mister Sturdy joined the riding party, and what Mister Sturdy didn't savvy about formations of rock, the different qualities of gold-bearing ore, and the how, where and why-for of all the big strikes, just wasn't worth a duck's teeth. What specially interested Rand was to watch Sturdy's behaviour in camp, when he smoothly reined in and steered the hot talk of Big Bruce. Even Symes responded to Sturdy's personality. But nobody would ever really master and subdue that cold-blooded killer.

Rand mostly fancied riding alone, naturally; and one time as he meandered through the intricate windings of the canyons, he had a queer experience. He had ridden further than usual and was about to turn back and head for camp when, rebounding from one gulch to another, came the crash of gunfire. Alarmed yet afire with curiosity, Jeff started to search around. But those lofty walls of rock, still echoing repeated shots, were a power of deception in themselves. One could get himself real scared by their resounding behaviour; and what with jerking and turning this way and that in the saddle, one could get a badly twisted neck, not to mention other slight diseases. Of a sudden the firing stopped, however, long before Rand injured himself or came any place near discovering its source.

Next day, deliberately riding through the same location, it all began again like a kind of ghostly ritual. Off went Rand, searching like mad; galloping recklessly down one rock strewn ravine, dashing all out into another, then branching off sometimes to cut along tight-squeeze fissures, and continuously making breathless halts to listen. It was downright exciting

56

while it lasted, and reminded him of hunting jack-rabbits with Jim Miller. And like Jim used to say: dogged perseverance has its reward. Only Rand's reward on the present occasion filled him with anxious dismay.

Finally he came along a narrow pass, wherein stood Jake Crocker, perfecting an already slick gun-draw. A hundred yards or so wide of Jake lay a heap of bullet-riddled cans, purposely lugged out there from camp. Plain to see, Jake was preparing in earnest to avenge his no-good brother. Rand watched the fellow's progress for close on an hour. Long before he stealthily departed, he had to admit that Jake Crocker was no slouch with a six-gun.

Strong now grew that desire to drift and avoid more bloodshed: Rand became as restless as the desert sands, and as he rode back to camp after his discovery, he more firmly resolved to ride off for good at nightfall. Nonetheless, when he struck camp again and headed straight for his sleeping quarters, quietly figuring out what supplies he would carry away with him, he made another find, a whole piece more astounding than the last.

It was stifling hot inside the cabin, and blinding dark after the sun's brilliance. Jeff, groping forward, stumbled first against a wooden wash bowl, or rather half a barrel, then tripped over a pair of saddle-bags. He cursed gently. He bent down to remedy the damage: from those saddle-bags tumbled toilet gear, cartridges, pieces of gold-veined rock, quids of tobacco – and Jim Miller's watch! Shock overwhelmed Rand. He grew pale and cold. Slowly and tenderly he picked up Old Jim's once cherished possession. It was Jim's all right. In a prayer-like murmur Jeff read the inscription, laboriously scraped on the back. It had once taken him a whole afternoon to perfect the lettering.

'To Jim, a great old friend, from Jeff.'

Bitter curses leapt to Rand's lips. Fiercely he hauled up the saddle-bags, his face twisted with intense hatred. Murderously he glared at the name branded thereon – William Sturdy.

How long Rand stood there, furiously pondering, he had no distinct idea. He mentally retraced the winding trail back across the flowing desert, past the time when Sturdy mentioned a certain prospector's gold-finding mules, and back through Vulch City; then beyond to those scorching plains, to the trails he had followed, and so into the woodland beauty of the mountains. Finally Rand arrived back to the hour of Jim Miller's death at the mine. As he had held Jim up in the creek, the dying old fellow had mentioned that about six men had raided the place, and that one of them had been smartly dressed in black, just like a judge. That's what Jim had said: just like a judge. It had been Sturdy. Sturdy, the genial and instructive Mister William Sturdy, guilty of murdering James Miller. Rand decided to kill him.

The sun was setting. Night was arising from the gullies below to the crannies above, and loading those lofty unexplorable places with a wilder mystery. A thin spiral of smoke was feeding a motionless halo that lay over Grapevine Gulch. The smoke issued from the main cabin, accompanied by mealtime sounds served up with a relish of profanity. That profanity was of a mirthless kind, due to the expectation of Clay riding in with good news from Flintstone.

No light shone from Rand's cabin. A glow of burning tobacco came and went at regular intervals in the gaping doorway, while a last blood-red shaft of sunset absorbed itself on the doorpost, like an omen of early Winter, or of sudden and terrible death. Jeff Rand was sprawled idly on a blanket, and he stared outside with a face as wooden as an Indian's. The all-revealing saddle-bags had been repacked, and once more held the old prospector's watch. Rand's first impulse

58

had been to pocket the timepiece, shock Sturdy with a sudden accusation, then with a challenge, and finally with death in a flaming gunfight. But now calmer reasoning controlled him. Rand smiled bitterly and mirthlessly as he heard Merrick and Sturdy approaching, wearily dragging spurred boots through the grass. They entered.

'Who's that? Say, you startled me, Jeff!' Sturdy grunted, angry because he had jumped. 'Guess moody fellas like skulking in dark places.'

'Shucks, you can't blame Jeff for steering clear of Gowl's stomach-howling hash,' chuckled Smily. 'Here you are, Jeff; I've rustled these wheatcakes and this bottle of rye for yuh. A man will perish to dust in the infernal heat here, unless he feeds on something.'

'Thanks, Smily,' Rand forced a grin, and his grins were rare, and therefore valuable to the worshipping Merrick.

'Hello-hell! Whose hoofmarks are these on my saddle-bags?' Sturdy now wanted to know, lighting the lamp and glancing over his property. 'Just cast a look at this mess, Jeff,' he went on, a humorous twist to his mouth as he displayed the marks of crime. 'Bet those mighty prints belong to Merrick.'

'Too dainty for him,' observed Rand, solemnly inspecting the saddle-bags. 'More like signs of a pack-mule to me.'

'Aw shucks, I'm sorry; I'm clumsy, Mister Sturdy. I reckon I ain't no lady. Seems my Pa was right; seems my feet have grown some.'

'Never mind, kid. They'll stop. The rest of yuh will catch up, I hope,' Sturdy consoled him, but with a gravity really disturbing to Smily.

Rand did not respond to Mister Sturdy's fun-making. In fact he no longer heard him. His mind was on gold, honest and hard-earned gold, equalling in his mind the promised share-out from the bank raid. Somewhere in this gulch lay a season's rich output of truly high quality ore from Miller's Mine. Once it was located and lifted Rand aimed to confront the killer. There would then be a different grin on the false face of Mister William Sturdy.

Rand resolved to begin his search as soon as the camp was wrapped in sleep. Sturdy and Merrick retired early; and when at last Sturdy quit smoking and slept, Rand still lay waiting. Hours seemed to pass. He watched the lamp burn itself out, then watched the moon's lazy-headed travel from one upper ridge to another. Eventually the moon so situated itself that the gulch became flooded by the mountain's black and thunderous-looking shadow. Rand arose.

Leaving his boots behind him, knowing he moved quieter and swifter on his bad foot without them, he glided outside, strapping on his gunbelt. He crossed over to the main cabin, bounding for its side like a hunting wildcat. Precisely as Rand leapt for that wall, a gunshot jolted his heart. He was discovered. But no! There was some other reason. Hoofbeats and the rattling slither of shale announced the arrival of some night riders. Next instant three horses could be distinctly heard thudding across the spongy turf, heading straight towards him.

'Clay!' one of the riders hailed the cabin. 'Wake up, you drunken fools! It's Clay, I tell yuh. Clay's back from town. The shipment's arrived. Roll out, you sluggards!'

A lamp flared up in the cabin. Rand shrank down behind a woodpile. A half-dressed figure burst forth, staggered, swore, and took a more supporting grip at the front of his pants.

'Dry up!' The figure bawled like a runaway bull. 'Who's a-yawling them words? Who's a-telling the whole derned world our bizness?'

' 'Sme, boss – Tom. Clay's here. Better saddle up – ride for Flintstone – raid the . . .'

Crunch! A sickening thud of fist contacting flesh, and followed by an agonised cry, brought silence.

Some minutes later the entire gang had crowded into the large cabin; and a more mixed looking group of fellows could scarce be imagined. Some swayed sleepily, others drunkenly, yet others tried to look intelligent in shirt-tails, round which they fumbled to tie gunbelts, and all spoke at once, demanding a clear account of affairs from Clay. Big Bruce thrust a mugful of liquor into Clay's wiry hands, then released a loud bellow for silence. Not another word came from any man.

'An outright plump shipment o' dollar bills. Seen it with my own eyes.' So stated Clay with an air of supreme importance. 'Yup, fellas, I ain't never seen so much. I was sweeping the saloon verandee at the time, and what a back-breaker that job was, when the stage pulled in all nice and neat as per usual. No extra guards, no nothing. Next thing I knows I saw the smarty boys from the bank bearing off a coupla hefty cases. It wasn't until sundown that Hank came over for his drinks, but this time he was red and excited, yeah, and nervous too. There was one thing about me, I ain't no nervous cuss like Hank. Anyhow, he sez the shipment's in, bigger than we ever expected; it was the bigness what was a-scaring him. Well, boss, that's the set-up.'

'What did Hank Williams say exactly?' Bruce demanded with angry impatience, brought on by Clay's conceited manner, for he sat on the table and sneered proudly at everybody.

'Hank jest sez it's a sure-fire thing, Mister Bruce.' Clay informed him, swilling his mouth from the mug and looking at the now greedily passionate faces staring at him. 'Look here, boys, don't make a breakneck dash for Flintstone, however. This needs careful handling. You all will get rich plenty, and soon enough.' Clay grinned, real generous like.

'Hank sez come Tuesday noon, slack bizness time. We've three days to make it.'

'Is that everything, kid?' Bruce suddenly roared at him, his hands moving restlessly.

'Yes, Mister Bruce. Yes, sir!' exclaimed Clay, stammering and stretching his scrawny neck.

'Want me to straighten out the youngster?' a cold and softly drawling voice crept from a certain bunk.

Clay, tightly clenching the mug in both hands, trembled audibly and retreated backward to the door.

'No, Symes,' sighed Bruce, glancing tiredly over his shoulder. 'And please quit foolin' with that gun. We'll be needing everybody for this job. It's a sight bigger than I ever thought. We'll ride tomorrow at sundown.'

Jeff Rand had remained in hiding outside the cabin, leaning close to the paneless window. On hearing those final words, followed by a maniacal laugh from Symes, he quietly moved away. As he did so another hidden figure moved into the lamplight slanting from the doorway. A shrewd smile played on Mister Sturdy's face as he watched Rand's soft-footed retreat.

CHAPTER SEVEN

Daybreak over Grapevine Gulch was both a picturesque and eerie spectacle. As the desert sun elevated itself with blinding splendour above the mountains, the sky became a mighty goldfield, while sand that had sometime drifted high along the gullies, looked like flowing rivers of gold. But an unearthly atmosphere, an awful waiting silence haunted that territory, in fact the land was like the long dead face of the moon.

Down in the gulch a tall figure, stripped to the waist and carrying a washbowl, sauntered forth from the smallest cabin. This early riser, after stretching and yawning and scanning the scenery, crossed to a spring which spurted from the mountain side. Having filled the washbowl and watered his horse, he retraced his steps, hung his gunbelt across a nail outside the cabin, and began to wash.

A few seconds passed, then another figure appeared, climbing stealthily to the summit of a small mound between the cabins. This fellow was already dressed, and, as he watched the person below, he grew peculiarly tensed and rigid of body.

'Hi, Mister Dirt! Washing ain't ever gonna clean away Ted's murder.'

The man stooping over the washbowl at once ceased to move. Those words, as they came stealing venomously behind him, were received with a queer thrill down the spine. He fought back an urge to swing around, knowing such a sudden action could cost his life.

'It's Crocker, ain't it?' he mildly inquired, taking a fleeting glance at his hanging guns, then secretly watching Crocker's reflection in a jagged piece of glass left hanging in the cabin window. 'Say, you rise early, neighbour; I guess you like a peaceful sun-up.'

'Listen, Rand. I said you'd never pack Ted's pay-roll, and you won't,' began Crocker, his voice starting to joggle in hidden depths of hatred.

'You listen, sonny,' cut in Rand, who now dare not budge an inch. 'I heard there's been a strike down in hell. So just hang around me, fella, and you'll sure get in a free claim.'

'I said I was gonna kill yuh, Rand,' Crocker proceeded, growing softer, crouching lower. 'Yeah – and here I am!'

Again Jeff Rand's eyes flashed anxiously to his guns. They hung just out of arm's reach. He would never make it and live. This Crocker kid was certainly determined to fix him for good; and no, one simply could not under-rate him, not after that display of private gun practice. Another thing, Crocker was now refreshed after sleep, so how much swifter might he be this morning. Once again Rand covertly studied the man's reflection. Jake Crocker's hand was already resting on his gun-butt.

'You don't figure on taking no chances, do yuh?' Rand observed with a low chuckle. 'Reckon you judge this the safest time to make your fight, me with guns off, hands all soapy, no other folk around, and me sun-blinded if I swings about.' Jeff continued talking with a lazy carefreeness. 'I think you're not a very kind hombre, son. You know what? I b'lieve you're a dirty low-down squirt!' His voice turned suddenly harsh and sinister.

Fiery wrath choked Crocker's utterance. He fixed madly boring eyes on Rand's back. He was ready. Still Rand remained motionless, head bowed, wholly relaxed, hopelessly surrendering to the execution. He saw the effect his final words had produced, and he knew the moment had come. One of his hands he had kept dry, yet in the other he held a slithery block of soap. He now tightly squeezed that block. The soap flipped leftwards. It caused a momentary distraction. Then it happened.

'Drag it!' Crocker seemed to shriek the words; and he dived into action.

A veil of blood seemed to pass across Rand's eyes. Down he sank: he flumped on his knees in the mud, and spun around in the same motion. In the same instant he dragged down his gunbelt. Before that belt slapped the earth Rand's gun was belching. Shots pounded and zipped to and fro. Crocker screamed first, then collapsed, three slugs tearing into his chest. Rand had grown pallid and expressionless. He continued to kneel, gun still directed, far extended, all in a kind of staring and staring trance. An oddly gurgling liquid was coursing round his knees. Two inches from Rand's brain, a bullet had bored through the washbowl.

A number of half-dressed men, first drawn outside by the sounds of the quarrel, had seen it happen. Now they stood gaping, stunned by the sudden explosions and the swiftness of death. Big Bruce, with a towel round his neck, outstretched half his body through a window, and with sagging underjaw he stared at the scene.

'Rand!' he presently called, sounding hoarse, gradually overcoming his shock. 'Thought I ordered no killing round here? Quit it, do yuh hear?' Bruce grew red, because his voice rattled nervously on those last words. He began to snort in mounting rage, and he kept sawing at his neck with the towel. 'Rand! Plug up that tomfool washbowl. Let other men wash, won't yuh? It makes me real mad to lose good men thisaway.

Hi you! Rand! Are you deaf? Fix that tomfool washbowl!' With a muttered curse Bruce jerked his head inside.

Before Rand arose, a movement at the nearby corner of the cabin caught his attention. He whipped about, gun cocked. There he saw Mister Sturdy, neatly dressed and holding a long-barrelled weapon under his coat. Following the direction which the weapon secretly pointed out he next noticed Symes. Throughout the whole incident since Jeff first appeared outside, Symes had been seated on a ledge above the gulch. Doubtlessly he had anticipated the performance, and risen early to take a ringside seat. Symes, noticing he was discovered, vented a devilish laugh. But what puzzled Jeff was Mister Sturdy's unexpected protection; and even when Sturdy echoed Symes' laugh, that hidden gun remained directed and ready to talk in a different humour.

'It looks kinda bad, Jeff, when a man can't wash in safety,' Symes yelled down, watching Rand arising and woefully regarding the muddy state of his weapons. 'Say, Jeff; how about that there strike in hell? I'm sorta interested, naturally. But I've a gnawing problem. If Crocker's now found rich diggings, how's he gonna wash his pay-dirt?'

Rand remained deaf to these and other jibes of the same nature, which Symes, chuckling continually, made as he climbed leisurely down to the gulch floor.

'I suppose I'm an inquisitive cuss, Jeff.' Symes released a long sigh as he stopped and smirked at Crocker's body. 'And also a cuss what packs special dislike for back-creeping gun-blasting skunks!' Malice entered his voice; he drew back his foot to kick the corpse.

'Stop that!' Rand commanded, snapping like a teamster's whip.

Another of those battles of looks resulted. 'Sure, Jeff. I'll quit. I'm amiable; I can deny myself for a friend like Rand,' laughed Symes. 'What a pity you had to waste such a load of lead, though; but never mind, the crow-meat's all yours, and easy come by. Actually poor Jake didn't stand a chance, being almost blind with tears for brother Ted.'

This cunning remark brought a low growling from the men. Rand watched them scowling darkly at him as he wiped his gunbelt.

'Still, it's a rotten shame you can't wash in peace, Jeff,' Symes repeated. 'Like me, you'll have to lead a dirty life, I figure.'

Symes began to approach Rand, swaggering and smiling broadly, and glancing up and down his mud-smeared form.

'A dirty fight, Jeff. A real dirty fight,' he mournfully whispered, shaking his head.

Just how fast with a gun was Symes? The question pulsed again in Rand's mind as he watched him pass by.

'I like you, Jeff. You're the easy type. Keep slugging and you'll make yourself a pile.'

Symes passed on a few more paces, suddenly recollected something, and looked back with one hand on his six-shooter and the other rasping his chin.

'By the way. Did I tell yuh to quit killing the boys? But sure, you'll quit. It would be derned shameful for me to kill you!'

No laughter, not even a grin came from Symes now. Turning stiffly he strolled away towards the horses.

'Rand!' Big Bruce was again stretching himself through the window, and his bawling betrayed a return of courage, caused perhaps by Symes' behaviour. 'Rand, don't let me ever catch you without those guns.' Bruce smote the window ledge with his fist. 'Now get that tom-fool washbowl fixed!'

'Do as the boss sez,' advised Mister Sturdy, solemnly picking up and holding out a piece of wood.

Rand turned and with puckered brow he fixed a thoughtful gaze on Jim Miller's killer. Meanwhile Smily Merrick stole from the cabin and took the offered piece of wood.

'Leave it to me, Jeff,' he whispered; and at once he began expertly to whittle a bung for the bowl. 'Fancy Jake making a dirty pass at you like that, Jeff. Poor fool.' Smily muttered half to himself, disappointed to have missed the gunfight, awed by the sight of death, and secretly hoping Rand might explain. 'Just how did it happen, I wonder?'

Nobody answered him. Mister Sturdy smiled grimly at Rand then gravely ordered two of the men to bury Jake, which burial he departed to supervise.

'Well, I never did like Crocker; a scorpion if ever there was one,' sympathised Smily, hammering in the bung.

Still Rand did not appear to hear him; expressionless of face, he kept watching a certain man who whistled blithely as he groomed his horse, and that man was Symes.

For the remainder of the morning Jeff Rand was absent; he had the diplomacy to take one of his lonely rides until peace restored itself to the gang. Maybe it would have been wise to have kept riding, never to return again, for if he had been disliked before, he was now deeply hated. The gunfight, Bruce's longing to punch his face out of recognition, Symes' cunning manner of turning every man against him, and above all Symes' last departing threat, should have been sufficient reasons for a quick ride into the running desert. Yet Rand could not do it, and live peacefully with himself afterwards. Sure enough he was uneasy, in fact right down scared, though by midday he was riding quietly back into Grapevine Gulch. The queer and unexpected behaviour of Mister Sturdy caused him much confusion, seeming to shatter his private plan. Why did Sturdy protect him? Did Sturdy really murder Old Jim Miller? Finally – where was that gold?

CHAPTER EIGHT

The Bruce gang drank thirstily at Clay's news of the outside world. They heard how Flintstone was booming, how a new saloon and chop-house had appeared in the last week, and how emigrants were arriving by the hundreds. Whisky, music, girls, gambling – entertainment no end was now possible in Flintstone: but the new sheriff was in dead earnest and the town was becoming refined. Folk even bathed at a special bath-house; one fellow, the president of Bulmer's Bank, did it every day. But other far more unhealthy extravagances were taking place; and despite some folk a-going to church come Sundays, and the wearing of boiled shirts on weekdays, the town was pretty much the same underneath, and just as rip-snorting as Deadwood. Sure enough, Flintstone was booming, and sure enough Bulmer's Bank was growing sinfully rich.

Big Bruce was likewise refreshed and encheered by Clay's lively gossip; and after the midday meal he summoned the whole gang outside. Leading the men to a smooth stretch of sand down the gulch, he proceeded to map out in detail the coming raid. All were told what positions and duties they would adopt on entering Flintstone; and all were given alter-native orders in the event of trouble arising. Everyone was made to comprehend that, after rushing the shipment of dollars out of town, the gang would divide, one company coming under Symes' command, the other following Bruce. Later both companies would unite at a different hideout.

The entire scheme sounded simple yet shrewd, and the men could not conceal their pleasure and admiration. Big Bruce felt their heightened respect for him, naturally; and so, with sheepish eyes straying to the mildly watching Mister Sturdy, he repeated the whole set-up. He then questioned members of the gang as if he were a kind of school ma'am, and soon got to bullying them with curses and threats of physical violence into remembering their individual parts. Yes, Bruce made most of his moment of glory, while Symes smirked insultingly at him, and while Mister Sturdy looked on with a tolerant smile.

In the meantime Smily Merrick stole towards the empty main cabin, where he borrowed a can of coffee and a plateful of beans and biscuits. Smily had seen Jeff riding back into camp, looking sadly haggard and hungry. Unfortunately Rand was carefully bandaging his bad foot, over which injury he was uncommonly sensitive, when Merrick entered with the food.

'Say, I didn't know Crocker had wounded yuh, Jeff!' Smily exclaimed, his eyes widening as he beheld Rand's foot.

'I didn't neither,' Jeff answered coldly.

'Can't see no blood though,' mused Smily.

'Yeah, it's a pretty dry do, ain't it?' said Rand.

'Guess that wound is old, huh?'

'A genuine antique,' replied Jeff, firmly tying the bandage and almost allowing himself to smile. 'Just don't talk it around the camp. There are some folk who would use another's weakness to advantage, if you see what I mean. Thanks for the grub, kid.'

Smily waved a hand and grinned, then stood pondering and rasping his chin.

'What's the pow-wow out there?' Rand carelessly inquired.

'Is someone punching Bruce's head?'

Within a few minutes Smily acquainted Jeff with all the information which, judging from the bawling and preaching, Bruce was repeating a third time in pursuit of vain-glory. Then once more Smily stood pondering, shifting his weight from one leg to another, finding no lasting support on either of them.

'Well, what's your problem?' Jeff finally asked him.

'Nothing much.' Smily looked embarrassed. 'I keep wondering how you managed it, that's all. They say Crocker drew first, and behind your back. And yet – well – see what I mean?'

With impressive slowness Rand raised his head from the coffee-can, whereat Merrick's words faded into silence. The boring regard of those pale blue eyes occasioned a strange thrill of fear.

'Still hankering to be a gun-slapper, eh, kid? Well, believe me, you're crazy. The life's hell on earth.'

Bitter and mournful and oddly far-away was the voice Rand used. He continued to stare through the man before him, and not once did he blink. Smily licked his lips.

'A fella just don't know what peace is till he loses it,' muttered Rand. 'Once you start drawing a gun, you stand alone agin the world. Decent folk fear and despise yuh. Black-hearted folk fear and hate yuh. And fools like Smily Merrick give you a false kind of honour.'

Another short interlude of grim silence came. The face of Smily had paled slightly; to him, at that moment, Rand had become a different and terribly frightening person, no less than if he confronted him as a killer with a gun.

'Listen, kid. When humanity gets to hating you out-and-out that way, you get real lonesome – you get scared. Sure you act tough, you play rough – mebbe you really are a hard fella. But you're still scared. You lay awake nights, worrying ways out of the hell-hole you're in, and thinking of men you killed, and

71

knowing their kinfolk are a-waiting somewheres to get yuh. So you're forced to stick, it seems, until the derned bitter end, till you're slugged in the back, by some fool kid seeking gun-glory.'

Smily writhed, and kept wiping the beads of sweat from his face. Rand's words seemed to be striking into his very private thoughts; and Rand's eyes seemed to be turning over his very soul, and sourly studying it like a rotten coin.

'A gunfighter's life is hell,' Rand repeated, softly with hidden passion, more awesome than if he bawled the statement. 'You've gotta plan all your moves, little things that have their own peculiar risks; things you do every day. That was where Crocker slipped up; and there was just one fact Crocker didn't know; that I had checked over all his chances of getting a drop on me. No, Smily Merrick; seek no gunfame, neighbour. It ain't for decent God-fearing men who wash with both hands.'

A sombre silence followed this outburst of Rand's, the longest stretch of talking he had made in years, so he felt. But suddenly, the far-away look vanished, and his eyes began to blaze at the awe-stricken Smily.

'Well, what's your trouble, Mister? Have your derned feet taken root? I said thanks for the grub. Now beat it!'

Smily Merrick retreated with interesting quickness. He had a lot of thinking to do. Rand sat alone, his coffee growing colder and colder.

It was the eve of the raid. The sun glared intensely across the rugged mountains, set the cacti crackling like it were afire, and caused a quivering heat even in the well-like depth of Grapevine Gulch.

Inside the cabins the tortures of suspense increased. Drinking and gambling and bickering, the men awaited the sundown. Mister Sturdy alone seemed sociable and the only man capable of soothing one's nerves, as he sat there in the main cabin, dealing out cards, relating humorous anecdotes, and delicately changing the conversation whenever passed raids and misfortunes were mentioned. That man Sturdy was a diplomat through-and-through. Nevertheless, the general mood of the gang grew dark and forbidding; nor were tempers lessened by the uncommon heat, or by a growing suspicion of each other. Less men, more money, bigger shares for Bruce and company – this was the thought fermented by the tortures of waiting. What were they wasting time for anyhow? The money was there, wasn't it?

'Look yuh here, Bruce. Me and Jim and Tom and Larry, we figure on taking no more chances of agin losing yon shipment. We've suffered enough already as it is, and ain't a-reckoning to hang around this lousy gulch no longer. It's wuss than jail, and that's flat. We are riding out, now!'

So stated Winters, a great hulking fellow with a perfectly bald head: he used to own a sawmill down South. But as Winters rose to leave, Bruce pounced, and proceeded to beat him into an awful bloody state, as if poor Winters had somehow got tangled with the works of his old profession. The scene only lasted five minutes, seeming hardly like one to Big Bruce as he waded in with downright pleasure, yet it had the ability to divert the gang who thirsted for any kind of entertainment. Nonetheless, the scene put an end to ideas of a mutinous nature, and left Winters unfit to support himself far less accompany a raid on one of the best fortified banks in the territory.

'I'm the boss; order-giving is my bizness. We leave at sundown!' panted Bruce, his restless feelings obviously relieved by the fistwork. 'Gowl, get this rotten hunk o' meat out of here; give it to the vultures if yuh fancy. Yeah, then pack your gear, Mister Gowl, and get riding for that new hideout at Sweetwater. Prepare to take in the boys, as we'll jine yuh in two days.'

The sun was declining when Gowl pulled out with a string

of pack-mules, all well-fattened; in fact those mules had packed away a suicidal amount of dinners since entering Grapevine, and Gowl thought it worse than towing a line of overloaded boilers, so stubborn were those mules. With Gowl went Clay and the badly-mauled Winters. The gang, thoughtful and quiet, had tumbled outside the cabin to watch the boys go; and they wondered in what changed circumstances and fortunes they would join them again. The party of three wound down the gulch and out through Rattlesnake Pass.

At long last the plan was in operation: the first move had been made.

Less sullen became the gang's mood. Wild inventions for the spending of the long anticipated dollars were exchanged between the men. Lounging on goods-boxes, crouching round the table, eyes glowing in swarthy sunburnt faces, they talked of real high living, of unrestrained luxury. Sam was extra keen on beginning a life that seemed to consist of oysters and champagne. Mex said he was a-going to fix up a trading post on the Mexican border, and if Sam happened to ride by anytime, then Mex was going to show him what living was really like, and to blazes with oysters and gut-rot. Tom, on the other hand, said he figured on setting up a gambling-house, after he had married a certain girl he had in mind. The old-timer with the tapering beard sneered at the champagne, and the oysters, and even the girl, but would not reveal just what he was a-going to do. In fact the old man's attitude roused everybody's curiosity real bad. Everybody felt the oldster was going one step better than them somehow. Everybody felt they too wanted to do whatever the mysterious something was. As they tormented him with questions and only got sly grins and 'never you minds' from the antique fellow, their indignation expanded and finally exploded. They cursed the old man until he was blue in the face, then they ignored him completely, and listened to Smily Merrick. With a wistful look Smily said he was intending to reclaim his pa's rangeland, specially now the desert was flowing back almost visibly, one inch after another. He would then build him a ranch-house, rescue his sister from that no-good honky-tonk in Fairgo City, and settle down to raising cattle. Yes, the mood of the Bruce gang grew a sight more friendly as the sun dropped exhausted over the mountains, yet underneath their amiable chatter the tension had abated none. In fact the tension was momentarily increasing, and when darkness began to creep up the sides of Grapevine Gulch, it eventually produced an almost insupportable hush.

'Air's a whole lot cooler,' commented Mister Sturdy in a strained voice.

'That's right. Best prepare your company to move out, Symes,' murmured Bruce, glancing at Mister Sturdy who solemnly nodded.

Symes and his boys swaggered out to the corral and, with idle curiosity, everybody followed to watch them saddle up.

Jeff Rand was seated alone in the doorway of one of the empty cabins. On seeing the men file outside, sudden realisation brought him upright. Here, perhaps, was his final opportunity to search yonder main cabin for his gold.

It was still considerably light, an evasive and deceptive light, a light which distorted objects inside the main cabin. The reek of tobacco, whiskey and sweat met Rand as he stealthily entered. He looked at the walls: they were solid, and one consisted of the mountainside itself, causing uneasy thoughts on the results of an avalanche. The floor was lava rock, and the plank roof offered no place to hide even a bottle. Only the tumbled heap of provisions, most of which Gowl was at present freighting across the desert, could possibly conceal the sacks of gold he sought. Rapidly and thoroughly Rand made his search, but all to no avail, except for the finding of one familiar leather pouch that had once contained a few nuggets. The letters J.M. were stained upon it. This at least was sound evidence of Jim Miller's gold once being hidden here. Could that fellow Gowl be trans-shipping the ore even as he searched? Then again, maybe Symes had cached it somewhere right nearby, say up in these very mountains.

As Jeff stood there pondering, suspecting first one then another, then everybody of that particular theft and murder, his gaze became abstractedly fastened on a broad and ominous gunbelt slung across a chair. Gradually it impressed itself upon his busy mind. Recognition came with a kind of shock: Symes' guns! He picked them up gently, if not somewhat fearfully, and felt at once their cold strangeness. He chuckled softly. This was interesting; this was very, very interesting.

First Rand was surprised by the heavy weight of the belt and the Colt Forty-Fives. An instant later his surprise became astonishment as he tested the draw of one gun. It seemed to stick stiffly at first – then, as from an uncoiling spring, the weapon flew back and up in his hand. At this he grunted, frowning, engrossed. A brief inspection revealed that the holster leather, tightly stretched over the cylinder, had uncommon elasticity. The device must give about an extra second's speed, so Jeff mused: and he continued to wonder how often that second had saved Symes' life. Letting the weapon slide back, he tried again. How smooth it was! He grinned; he was more deeply intrigued and determined to come by some of this high quality leather. Once more, now with lightning rapidity, Rand drew Symes' six-shooter.

'Having fun, Jeff?'

A voice drawled in the open doorway.

76

CHAPTER NINE

Rand spun around as if challenged. His own gun appeared in his hand as though by strange power. Symes' face changed, and his gaze alternated between his own weapon and the stony-faced gunman.

Inwardly Rand was cursing himself for his inquisitive behaviour, as well as for his subsequent hastiness. His hostile action had created a grim deadlock.

'Play with fire and you get burnt, Jeff,' whispered Symes, licking his lips and rubbing his hands along his empty waist. 'Sling across them guns, Mister Snoop. Give me an even chance. Or are you scared?'

The muscles contracted and twitched on Rand's neck. Now the men were gathering around the doorway, and muttering in alarm.

'Rand's got the drop on Symes,' he heard Tom say.

'Never did trust Rand, not me. Him dark and gloomy man.' growled Mex. 'He ain't fair with the guns. He murders Crocker boys, and if we don't . . .'

'Pack that talk, Mex,' rapped out Smily Merrick, 'Jeff is a square fella.'

'Sling me my guns!' Symes was growing white, striving to suppress his eagerness.

Jeff lifted and hurled the belt and guns. They struck Symes upon the chest; Symes gasped and staggered at the unexpected impact. First he looked pained, then shocked, next relieved, and finally furious. Glaring malevolently he buckled on his belt.

'Interested in my hardware, are yuh?' he breathed, his lips a straight line and the cords of his neck standing out and throbbing. 'All right, if you want a demonstration, just stuff back your gun, mister, and we'll entertain these boys.'

Rand holstered his weapon, to Symes' further amazement, and stood looking mildly at him.

'Well, draw the thing, yuh dirty fool,' hissed Symes.

'Why?' Rand inquired without emotion.

The question at once baffled Symes; the man's calm self-possession before him was something he had never before experienced. As he thought of it his passion cooled. Their war of looks continued a few seconds longer, until Symes started to chuckle: soon he was roaring in ridiculous mirth. Everybody else looked on with open-mouthed gravity, with the exception of Rand who, leaning idly against the wall, hooked his thumbs in his belt, kept blinking his eyes, and studying Symes as if he suffered from a pitiful mental disorder.

'You're a joker, Jeff. Yep, a real joker,' Symes declared. 'Appears like I grow careless with these irons o' mine, leaving 'em hanging around.'

'It ain't a mistake I advise you to repeat,' Rand reproached him.

'What's that?' Symes' good humour vanished, no less than if he had found himself afire.

'Stick to your guns, fella. They are your arms, legs and everything to yuh,' Rand murmured softly. 'You just don't leave limbs hanging around, I notice, so why leave them guns.'

'Your dead right, Jeff.' Symes was chuckling again. 'This is the first time I've been so long without these Forty-fives.'

'Let it be the last,' cautioned Rand. 'Because I always carry mine.'

Giving another forced laugh and shrugging his shoulders Symes whirled around to leave. But this action, made with characteristic impetuosity, collided him with Smily Merrick, who was craning his neck to catch a glimpse of Jeff inside.

'Cuss yuh!' Symes snarled, staggering: his harnessed rage broke loose completely.

'Sorry, pard, sorry!' sang out Smily, comically prancing aside. 'Never was a good hand at square dancing, not me, no, sir.'

'I'll square dance yuh. Your horrible ugly face always did make me sick, now it just turns my dern-blast stomach!' Then, uttering a filthy oath, Symes felled him with a back-handed slash across the face. 'Some smart folk round these parts need an example, and so I'm minded to drill yuh, kid. You're nothing but a wheedling son-of-a-sidewinder!'

Gasping and shaking, Smily scrambled to his feet. His lips would not stop trembling, no matter how hard he tried to control himself. A red blotch stood out lividly on his whitened face.

'I – I – said sorry, my mistake, Mister Symes. Hey, fellas, didn't I say sorry my mistake?'

The men bowed their heads, rubbed their grisly jaw-bones, and looked covertly at each other. No one answered poor Smily's appeal.

'Hain't you got ears, you skinny runt?' Symes goaded him. 'Didn't you hear me say you're a spineless whelp?' Symes was speaking more softly, confidentially, and with a leer of antici-pation. He folded his arms and waited.

The heart and soul of Smily Merrick was plainly in throes

of extreme torture. Sure he carried a gun; sure he could shoot straight – but not against a killer – and certainly not against the devil himself, Mister Symes. Smily still kept glancing round at his hushed and nervously on-looking buddies. He watched them disbelievingly as they shuffled slowly backward before his appealing looks. Why did they turn their heads away? They knew he was in the right, didn't they? Hadn't anybody any feeling for him? Surely they didn't think Symes would really – really . . . Merrick's restless gaze settled on Jeff Rand lounging in the cabin doorway. Yes, yes, Jeff could help him? But wait! Would Rand do anything after already backing down before Symes? Good lord, no; not much likelihood of that! He was trapped, helplessly caught in a gunfight – with SYMES!

'Stubborn cuss, ain't yuh? Surely you won't show yourself up before all these men, Mister Merrick?' Symes provoked him again. 'Say, what do you carry that iron for? Pull it, kid. I know you hate me worse than snake-juice. So come on, kill me. Or are you really a boneless rat?'

Nothing happened. The whole situation was still incredible to the good-natured Merrick. He stood stupefied, ashake with naked fear, until Symes, speaking in an oddly changed voice, made a terribly foul allusion to Smily's mother.

'Stop that! Quit it, Mister! Don't ever say that agin.' Smily's tremulous whisper was clearly audible in the deep hush.

'Why, sonny? What's the penalty?' Symes was thoroughly enjoying the situation. 'She was, wasn't she? Your ma, I mean.'

'Just – just look you here, Mister,' stammered Smily, his eyes flashing excitedly. 'Don't push us fellas too far. We want no trouble with you or nobody. Ain't that right, boys? No, sir'ee. I'm just kindly asking you to haul back that right down awful insult.'

An infuriating burst of mirth came from Symes. It subsided

with equally shocking suddenness. With gloating contempt he sneered at Merrick, and said:

'I'm sure a-begging your pardon, sonny. But I still think it is true, see?' Here again Symes repeated the terrible insult.

'Shut up!' Smily's fury was bursting despite himself. 'Keep your dirty mouth closed! You do it deliberately. There's a devil in yuh, mister.'

That was enough; no more was needed. It was more than a man could live down. But maybe – Smily brooded heatedly – maybe he could beat the fellow, drawing his gun first. Right was might, and by heaven he had a load of it on his side! Yeah, maybe he could rid folk of this poison known as Symes. Perhaps he could show these other scared jack-rabbit gang, Rand included, that he was not just a frightened young man. But he was; he admitted it privately – he was scared. Still, hadn't Jeff said everybody felt that way, even himself? Smily slowly turned sideways, his hand hovering over his gun. After all, he was younger than Symes, and by nature he was quick of movement. Yes, it wasn't really hard, nor a complex thing at all. You just darted a few inches, about three little inches, then lifted the barrel a fraction, and – well – there you were!

The leer had spread on the face of Mister Symes. He very slowly repeated his insult.

'You just can't speak to decent folk with them awful things in mind, Mister,' Smily mumbled, trying to keep an apologetic tone out of his voice.

But the sight of the professional killer, firmly standing there with his broad gunbelt and protruding guns, grew momentarily more unbearable, and seemed to loom nearer and fill Smily Merrick's landscape.

Closely he watched the killer's eyes, like Jeff had one-time advised him; and he tried to be relaxed, also like Jeff advised. Though every time Smily managed to believe he was relaxed, a giddy fear rocked him, bracing him back again in redoubled tension. Therefore he tried to think of other things: his mind, however, was like a roped steer, thrown, locked, entranced in dread of slaughter. For what seemed a long time Symes did not move, then suddenly his eyes changed: they narrowed and gleamed fiercely in triumph, and took a sidelong look at Jeff Rand. Thereupon, seeing his chance, Smily did it.

He dipped his hand. His gun was out, was raised, was levelled, and yet – yet Symes' attention was only just returning. Smily gasped; he had won; he had him. Symes was still stupidly waiting. It all happened in seconds. Smily's gun exploded – and yet. . . . Why, it was like a miracle!

A thunderous roar of gunfire, a stream of repeated shots ripped from the hands of Mister Symes. At that same instant, arising from Symes' interior, came a laugh whose ringing, fiendish quality chilled the blood. Now his guns, empty, breathing smoke, were again snugly holstered, seeming innocent. So swift, so sudden had been his action, that it was barely credible. But there lay the evidence of it – sudden death.

The men stood petrified. None could believe it had happened; none could grasp immediately that yonder lay – not Symes as was finally expected – but Smily Merrick. His face was just – just horrible, ripped brutally out of recognition!

'Good God!' someone exclaimed, the trembling voice, raised in genuine prayer, adding fresh awe and dread to the tragedy.

Jeff Rand stood dumbstricken, his face drawn and sickly. His hands were white and lean as he clenched at the doorpost. Wide-eyed he peered at Symes who leered victoriously back at him. Then, with a horrified expression, Rand stared at Smily's dead body.

Natural rebellion surged up within Rand, knowing Symes had killed from spite to strike at him. All too late Jeff realised what had been his true feelings for Smily Merrick: the young fellow had been his friend, the only one he had in this wretched gang. The knowledge engulfed Rand in an unknown fear, because he felt he should do something about it. But more shocking than anything else, came the understanding that, only a few moments ago, he had dared to goad Symes, to play tough with a devil-assisted killer, a gunfighter whose speed was – was simply indescribable, stunning. He, Rand, would have been that poor bleeding corpse. The thought sent a cold shudder through his heart.

For perhaps the first time in his lonesome life, Jeff became a victim of complete fear. A queer haze kept blurring his vision; a choking sensation in the throat set his chest heaving: and the men looked at him and waited, all expecting him to do something. Passionately he yearned to kill Symes at that moment; but no, he could not. Thought of it set him quaking and recoiling inwardly. Trance-like he continued to stare at the body and the killer.

'Hi there! Hi, you mad fools!' a voice hailed them, shrill with fury. 'What the shooting about? Do you boys think this a fine time to celebrate or something?'

Big Bruce rushed over with two men from the corral. His face was puffed with anger, though it deflated and its colour drained away on noticing the body.

'Say, what's that?' he breathed with characteristic stupidity. Next moment his eyes flashed upon Rand at whom he roared like a bull in a prairie fire. 'You! Drat you, Rand, what in tarnation you recken this is? So we have more of your handy shooting, huh? Another good man gone west. Now you're for it. I'm just waiting to find yuh without them guns, Mister, and then you're finished.'

A long jocular chuckle caused Bruce to whip round. Whereat he found Symes calmly thumbing cartridges into the chambers of his Forty-fives.

'Drew his gun fust; jest a crazy kid,' Symes explained, very regretful, in a very lazy manner. 'Can't noways figure what got into the fella; touch o' the sun, I guess. Lucky I'm alive, Bruce. Ain't that so, Rand?'

An answer to that question was more than Rand fancied to try at the moment. He deliberately fixed his attention on his boots, knowing it to be the safest thing to do, even if Symes did find it highly entertaining. Rand knew that neither himself, nor any man he had ever encountered in action, could equal Symes' gun-speed. It was a bitter admission, but Mister Symes was a slick-practised streak of lightning.

The boss had quickly mastered his rising anger, and summoned an unconvincing grin to meet the situation, all the while trying to appear unaware of Symes' sidelong look of challenging inquiry.

'Whose bundle o' rotten bones is it then?' Bruce asked, seeking to hide his fear under brutal words.

'It's Smily Jack Merrick,' Tom revealed in a gentle graveside voice.

'Oh, just Merrick! Well, that's different. I thought mebbe it was somebody. Serves him right. Caught a gunslinger's disease from Rand, I wager.' Bruce posted Rand a foreboding look. 'Tom and Mex, get the thing buried, won't yuh? We can't stand looking at this mess all night, there's a job to do, remember. As for you, Symes, don't let the matter worry you none. You're not a fella to waste lead for nothing. Mount up and lead your boys into Flintstone.'

'Leave that corpse alone!'

Mister Sturdy gravely strode from the rear of the gathering. Whether or not he had witnessed the incident, none could say, and none could calculate what his feelings were from his poker-face. He bent down and lifted Smily Merrick with a peculiar father-like tenderness, somewhat disturbing to Merrick's one-time buddies who coughed and bowed their heads. Sturdy called back over his shoulder, saying:

'Rand, come along with me. Ain't it about time you were riding, Symes? Like Bruce told yuh, we'll hit town about an hour after you and your party. Are you coming, Rand?'

It was with a cheerful wave and chuckle that Symes swung away, leapt into the saddle, and herded his boys away.

As the first party of riders galloped down the gulch and into the onrushing night, Bruce and the remainder of his gang re-entered the main cabin. Simple and superstitious as many of them were, this second visit of death had temporarily quelled the heartening prospect of a rich raid. Many accepted the killing as a forewarning of worse disaster.

The drumming of hoof-beats faded into the distance. Mister Sturdy, with Smily Merrick's bleeding body still cradled in his arms, stood immobile; and beside him, with outward signs of a person still suffering from shock, stood Jeff Rand. Both men stared down Grapevine Gulch.

CHAPTER TEN

Flintstone was well ahead for a two-year-old city. It originated when Jacob Rispin discovered gold where the creeks merged into Wawa river. But now Jacob's lucky strike had passed out of the placer stage into lode mining; now quartz mills were arriving at the diggings and now Flintstone was receiving hundreds of emigrants a week, so that any drifting saddle-tramp would scarcely recognize the place from month to month. Solid and substantial buildings, magnificent saloons with long mirrors and paintings, great storehouses loaded with tons of provisions, weekly trains of prairie freighters, everything that conduces to a rapid growth of wealth – such was Flintstone: and next to the largest saloon the most frequented place was Bulmer's Bank.

Upon the particular day under consideration, the dawn found Flintstone a right down peaceful and inviting town. It was only five a.m., however, and as usual the place had been turned into bedlam until two a.m. Admittedly the bedlam had not been so outright bad with the new sheriff in town, yet sufficient crime had been committed as could only be expected in a full-blown capital city. Nonetheless the shooting, so it was said, was hardly considered dangerous unless there had been intent to kill, and unless a fellow could prove his mind had not been unbalanced by liquor or good-luck at the time. Still, it was really marvellous just how many fellows had been getting lucky lately, were becoming strike-happy, and loosing high-spirits through their gun-barrels.

Six a.m. Now the main street was gradually giving signs of life. It was strange but the town was usually fully half-alive by this hour. Maybe there was nothing wrong, though; maybe in another hour or so the place would become the usual milling mass of miners, villains, women, kids, dogs, horses and wagons. Soon the bull-whackers would be cursing, oxen bawling, whips cracking, saws rasping, hammers rapping, and all the busy confusion of a Southwest town in painful growth would be a-loading that peaceful landscape. The minutes dragged by. Nothing seemed to happen. The still air seemed to be waiting to carry the customary hullabaloo, but it did not come. It was now exactly six-thirty a.m. This was getting serious. In actual fact it was already alarming.

The sun had risen vividly, too vividly, and a blistering heat had seeped at once into the already hard-baked earth. Under the slanting rays the town became a straggling mass of bright sides and glum shadows, shimmering and painful to the head: the customary touch of early morning freshness was absent. No dew, just ankle-deep dust awaited the breeze. Business was opening up lazily; citizens began to come abroad tiredly. The uproar slowly began, yet it reached nowhere near its accustomed peak. What was more astounding the tumult started to decline again. The heat, the energy-sapping heat grew more intense. It was unbelievable that there was any place so hot and airless this side of Hades. By noon an uncommon lethargy had gripped that booming gold-mining town of Flintstone.

There were lizards gasping in the cart-ruts and chasing flies along veranda rails. There were hardly any patrons in the twin lines of stores, except the saloons, whose bars were lined with silent groups of panting, gulping miners. Just a few drooping knots of horses were tied up at the hitching racks, with sunshine gleaming glossily over their quivering hides. Now scarcely any citizens appeared down that sweltering shimmering channel of hell called a street. Even the justice courts had closed down; even the over-crowded jail was silent like a forgotten church. Finally, the newly-arrived miners of last night, and the first hopeful early-risers of today, came straggling back into town, saying the diggings had hung-fire, beaten down by the heat.

'Hot enough to shrivel snakes,' commented the barkeep at the First Class Saloon. He dabbed his brow and surveyed his slim line of customers, all dusty, red and haggard. 'Yeah, I recollect last year when it got so derned hot, fellas, that rocks split like roasted nuts, and yella ore oozed out like likker.'

'You don't say!' exclaimed the tallest patron, hitching up a broad gunbelt as he added a boisterous laugh. 'Me and my boys here are used to hot places, pard.'

'Then you must be tough,' chuckled the barkeep.

'Real fire-eaters, Mister,' added the tall stranger, winking at his companions then leering challengingly at the astounded bartender.

Certainly the heat was fraying everybody's temper. Even the usually amiable old-timer in the hardware store across the street, next to Bulmer's Bank, was irritable.

'So it's high quality leather you want, young fella?' The old man scowled at his darkly-clad customer who, stretching a piece of leather and minutely inspecting it, kept a maddeningly blank face. 'Well, that's the best leather in town.'

'Are you really sure? Its derned important that I get the very best,' murmured the customer, limping slightly as he examined other sheets of hide hanging from the rafters.

'Look you here, I knows my bisness. What do you reckon you're a-holding, a piece of steak?'

'Shucks, don't get sore, Grandpa,' soothed the stranger,

grinning. 'This piece feels strong and pliable, sure enough.'

'What did I tell yuh?' snapped the old fellow. 'Why, you couldn't jab a fork into gravy off it.'

'Good. Give me a square foot of the stuff, Grandpa.' said the customer.

'What? Is that all!' The old fellow grew red with indignation.

'Yeah, that's all. I don't fancy big dinners on hot days. They put me in a killing mood.'

The old-timer looked staggered. Hastily he completed the sale, slicing the leather with fearful eagerness after the stranger had measured it across his holsters.

'Hot! Why, it's blood heat, boiling blood heat; tornado atmosphere. Do you know what? You bunch o' boys are my fust arrivals today.' So complained the owner of the general goods store, at the other side of Bulmer's Bank. 'You'd think a doggone plague had hit town, and half the folk were laid low with itchy-back or summat.'

'Is that the best chewing baccy you stock, Mister?' asked the foremost customer, adjusting the cuffs of his black lawyer-like suit.

'None better, friend, none better any place. Try some, it's the rarest shipment we've had.'

'Reckon you're right,' agreed the buyer, biting at a piece and spitting it out in terror. 'Good Lord Harry! It's a wonder it doesn't rear up, stagger out, and spread fever!'

A roar of laughter came from the speaker's buddies who, grinning at the amazed storekeeper, slowly filed by the counter, making small purchases.

It was shortly after noon when a large and well-dressed gentleman issued from the best hotel in town. Similar to other such persons occasionally seen in Flintstone, he gave the impression of a rich speculator arrived from the east, who doubtless owned and managed scores of rich mining properties. He was sleek, smoked a costly cigar, fanned his beefy red face with a silk handkerchief, kept wiping the inside brim of his expensive hat with same, and grinned magnanimously at the world as he swaggered along the plank sidewalk. Behind him, carefully keeping at a respectful distance, came four subservient associates neatly dressed like a set of aspiring undertakers, and carrying extraordinary weighty-looking saddle-bags. As the party passed the First Class Saloon it aroused the accustomed curiosity inside, and loud remarks that some greedy easterners would stay trading in any weather, and even go to hell to exploit Old Mischief.

This particular sally from the barkeep pleased his line of patrons, though in his enthusiasm to make his wit famous he had spoken just a little too loud. The gentleman outside halted abruptly, seemed to bloat hotly with indignation, then turned to scowl aggressively over the batwing doors. Everybody pretended to be unaware, especially the bartender who polished industriously at the counter. The man outside recollected himself and marched onward with an air of supreme disdain for the lower class. On passing a dry-goods store he gave a dollar to a squaw, who stood hungrily regarding certain melons and bunches of corn. Glowingly conscious of his own generous nature, the man then relit his cigar with a pompous flourish and swaggered across the street. He glanced over his shoulder and crooked a fat finger at his solemn followers. They entered the bank.

The main saloon disgorged a number of its patrons who strolled idly across the street, joking together. Two kids in bare feet and shirts ran out of the livery-stable, carrying a jar with a lizard in it, and followed by a stream of angry language. Ten seconds later a lanky rider walked his horse in the shadows while tying a roll of something to his saddle. The broad brim of his hat flapped up and down at each step he took, so he removed it and pinned the brim back as he passed the general store. There was a baby crying forlornly somewhere among the cabins by the creek. A group of tobacco-chewing customers sauntered forth from the store and headed up the street.

'Never seen the like o' this town today,' an old prospector mused to himself as he sprawled in the shade of a woodpile. 'There jest ain't nothing doing. And no blamed wonder,' he went on, watching the resin bubbling from the logs. 'If heat like this kills Flintstone, makes it gorgeous peaceful, then I'll go to hell.' He flicked his hat back over his face, and went to sleep.

Bulmer's Bank was the most substantial building in town, and its appearance with iron-clad doors and barred windows, was more suited to a prison. Inside everything was highly polished and smart, with horsehair couches along the walls, and a good-sized spittoon at every footrest beneath the counters, so that no fellow had any excuse whatsoever. Just to enter the place made one feel downright respectable, even nervously good-mannered, and keen to tie-up business quickly so as to relax and be natural again outside. The central counter supported a huge glass frame, curved, and holding the letters 'GOLD DUST.' Behind this stood a massive set of scales, behind which crouched a spruce clerk with waxed moustache, who kept calling out figures to a studious cashier away in a corner. Other learned fellows were visible bobbing up and down over ledgers in the Express Office. Such was Bulmer's Bank, most famous in the territory. A man felt ashamed to enter with less than fifty dollars, and sorry to come out empty-handed if luck was low at the diggings. Comparatively speaking, today the place was dead.

The big and dignified easterner had swaggered inside with his four attendants, waited until two or three sad-faced miners had finished their business at the Gold Dust counter, then approached with a wide grin. He rapped with strange loudness on the glass. Other visitors appeared stealthily. The Express Office doorway became blocked by a party of men who argued softly about the output of ore at the creek, while a tall fellow with a broad gunbelt kept shaking his head in contempt of their argument. The main doorway seemed to have become suddenly obstructed by a legal-looking man who instructively read aloud a notice of law-and-order pasted on the window. But the small side entrance contained one tall and sombre rider whose face looked dead as he lounged against the wall. The long anticipated hold-up was in operation. Bulmer's Bank was unconsciously in the clutches of the Bruce Gang.

Jeff Rand looked shocked and pale, as if he had just now realised the truth, that he was an accomplice in a bank raid which, if it succeeded, would go down in history as the biggest crime of its sort in the Southwest, and be talked of long after the raiders were buried and forgotten.

'Hi there, sir! Weigh me in for this load of ore, please. I'm a-fixing on opening an account here. The name's Bruce Crater.'

It was the boss speaking, and his voice thrilled every other man who made a pretence of being disinterested.

Big Bruce made a significant flourish with his cigar. His four followers tramped forward, sweating and panting. They emptied the saddle-bags on the counter. The amount and super quality of the gold widened the clerk's eyes. But the tall rider standing at the side-entrance was the most impressed. Everybody heard him gasp and brace himself, with a creaking of leather and a jingling of spurs. What was wrong with Rand? Was he going to ruin everything? Was he sick? Had he seen a ghost. But no; Rand only saw those sacks of ore, and each sack bore the initials J.M. Here at last and all too late, Jeff Rand had found Jim Miller's gold.

CHAPTER ELEVEN

A flaming wrath surged in Rand, and set him instinctively fingering his guns. But he could do nothing. Heated feelings subsided before a cold flood of disappointment. His gold was gone forever. The clerk behind the scales called excitedly for Hank Williams, the gang's assistant employed in the Express Office. Hank skipped forward briskly, and was told to speak to the president, to make an emergency appointment for a Mister Bruce Crater. Hank obediently disappeared through an office doorway immediately behind him. Rand licked his lips, his eyes darting this way and that, searching for an opportunity even now to grab his gold and run. The ruthless murder of Miller had a cunning motive behind it; this gang had needed a rich bait for the present raid, a bait not only rich but lifted at a safe distance from the gold-diggings at Flintstone.

Hank Williams reappeared to summon the big easterner into the president's office. Despair struck Jeff as he watched the four assistant-fellows regather the dead man's gold, that long-sought and honest-earned little fortune of poor Jim Miller. Rand could almost have sobbed as his rage mounted once more, and only by a supreme effort did he refrain himself from lunging forward with furious accusations and flaming guns. The four attendants followed Bruce and the clerks into the office. Bruce's pompous style had seemed comical to Rand before, though now it irritated him indescribably as he watched him meet the president, and the president was seated behind a wide desk, dressed lavishly, over-fed, and beaming magnanimously with greedy expectation. Rand caught a glimpse of iron-barred cells behind the desk, while the president extended a big hand to Mister Bruce Crater. The door closed. Then it began: an ordeal of waiting, an interior torment of tension, a sweating and a choking in a suspense only equal to a lull before a battle.

The big clock on the wall ticked the seconds with increasing loudness; the streaking of pens grated on ones nerve; the large fan circling in the middle of the ceiling kept sighing like a person in the agony of dying. Perspiration trickled down Rand's chest and sparkled on the backs of his lean, well-kept hands. Under the prolonged waiting it grew more and more difficult for the gang to keep its innocent masquerade of curious visitors conning the rules and regulations on the doors and walls. Silence, throbbing and nerve-wracking, gradually roped them all in; and every man's head kept turning in anxious expectation to the president's door, and to the bowed heads of the clerks. The Bruce Gang, in spite of all previous instructions, was beginning to break and give sign of its evil intention.

'Next, please! Look sharp there! Come on! Can I help any of you mining boys? This ain't some saloon you men can lounge around in. Who is next?'

It was the cashier who finally addressed them, raising a puzzled face from his ledger, sighing between words and mopping his hot neck. They all looked at him with mingled expressions of uneasiness, contempt and hate.

'Say, are you all together? Are you – you – you . . .'

They fixedly watched him become motionless, the hand-kerchief to his throat where his irritable words trailed into horrified choking noises. He was a small, hunch-shouldered and nervous man ordinarily full of suspicions, and sharp to discover anything amiss.

'What the hell? What goes on here?'

The gang was striving to recapture its look of careless inno-cence; the men grinned then scowled darkly and, like Symes who was about to load the cashier with hot lead, gradually assumed a violent mood. Mister Sturdy made a brave effort to save the situation, by first startling everyone with a burst of cheerful laughter.

'Seems you've gotten yourself a bunch of well-mannered callers, neighbour, who won't step one man afore another's turn. Sure I'll be next. I'm not heat-struck so's I cannot recollect my business with you, neighbour.'

Mister Sturdy sauntered forward, raising his hat to Symes and his boys.

'Hi-dee! Kind of hot, mister. Hopes you'll excuse my hurry as I have a horrible bad thirst flaming at my heels.' He stopped at the counter and leaned forward, wagging his hat before his face and breathing warmly on the partly reassured cashier. 'Listen, buster, my affairs are only fit for your president's ears. Understand?'

'Yes, yes. Confidential. I understand yuh,' mumbled the cashier blinking rapidly at the hat-waving, legal-looking gent. 'But the boss is busy just now. Best make a special appoint-ment.'

'It's this away, buster. I represent the Penrose Federation of Miners,' began Mister Sturdy in a real slick and admirable style while glancing round airily at Symes and company. 'Yeah, and due to pitched battles atween certain mine owners and strikers, I'm a-going to organize one of our peace-bringing branches in your overheated city. Now these sulky boys behind me here. No, not that bunch of idlers; these fellows here.'

'Yes, yes. I understand, sir,' lied the warmly confused cashier, twisting from side to side.

'Well, we want to pow-wow with the president of this bank. We want a copy of returns from certain grades of ore from certain mines hereabouts. I carry written permissions.'

'You'll have to wait, mister,' the cashier told him, not much convinced by all the talk. 'Can't say as I ever heard of bad blood at the diggings, or of any grouching miners since Jacob Crispin fust struck rich seams here. The men get large dividends, and the owners can easily meet expenditures, heavy as they are. You boys are all wrong.'

The crafty cashier gleamed round suspiciously at all the hard, tensed and narrowly watching faces – and he noted that not a single man there wore mining garb.

Mister Sturdy, maintaining a smile that was obviously paining his jaw-bones, continued to represent the Penrose Federation of Miners in high and haughty terms: but it got him nowhere with that naturally doubting man. Even while Mister Sturdy rattled on, reciting some of the good work of the federation, that cashier edged away. There was a sudden gleam of understanding in his little eyes. He darted like a jack-rabbit for the president's office. The sudden move left the gang confused. Sturdy had made a grab but all too late. Nobody could do anything; to shoot would rouse the whole town.

The other clerks had given attention to the proceedings at first, until Mister Sturdy had announced his business, whereafter they had carried on with their clerical duties, half-dazed by work, late dinners and the sweltering weather. They did not witness the cashier's behaviour, his sudden change, gasp of fear, and final retreat. Maybe the shock had struck the fellow speechless, for he uttered no word of alarm as he reached the president's door. He flung it open. Everyone of the gang saw the scene inside that office: everyone could see Big Bruce wrenching, gasping in fiendish fury as he strangled the president. One clerk lay dead across the broad desk, with Hank Williams' knife in his heart. The four attendant raiders were working busily behind the bars, unlocking the safes. Only for one moment did the door remain open. Then the terrified cashier, open-mouthed in his shock, was swept inside by Hank before he could sound the alarm. The door closed softly. A moment passed. A sickening thud reverberated through the building. The clerks outside all looked up, inquiring looks on their faces. Hank Williams immediately appeared, briskly rubbing his hands. He yawned and nodded to the clerks, who shrugged their shoulders, involuntarily yawned back, and exchanged signs to the effect that the president was in a rip-snorting bad mood. Hank at once greeted Mister Sturdy in a breezy and business-like style. Together they discussed the Penrose Federation of Miners, with a loudness which tortured the other brain-flogged officials, and a few newly-arrived miners passing through the Express Office with lists of rules they struggled to read. Although the gang's relief was great, it was certainly not complete. After what they had seen through that office door, every passing second became a private little hell, hotter than the last, and all boiling up the danger.

The waiting seemed unending; the strain was becoming unbearable. Unless Bruce and his boys came out soon, something disastrous would surely happen. The heat and pent-up feeling got mixed up tremendously, until one could feel one's heart and brain and every vein pulsing like mad. What in tarnation was keeping that big fool? Had something gone wrong inside there? Had the bank guards, who hadn't appeared nowhere, left the saloons, their cabins, or wherever they were, and sneaked in by the rear? Maybe it wasn't this dratted heat that kept folk at home, kept that town quiet, the bank empty, and those tomfool clerks dozing at their work. Was it all a trap? Perhaps the front of this bank was covered even now by every citizen able to carry a Winchester. Yeah; maybe the miners from the diggings were lined up, merely awaiting them to step outside, there to cut them down by a shattering volley.

The strong sense of alarm hushed the discourse between Mister Sturdy and Hank Williams who pretended to be pondering an account book on the counter. For some reason the great fan had quit swirling; the creaking of pens had stopped and the clerks were gazing round with worried looks. All tended to break the nerves of the more sensitive members of the gang. Tom was first to draw his gun, slyly hiding it in readiness behind a flap of his rawhide coat. Symes had tensed, half-crouching, ready to give the signal which would bring a roar of sudden death. Just as he raised his hand to blast that row of clerks into eternity, the door opened.

'Good day, Mister Bummel!' Bruce bawled jovially as he swaggered forth from the president's office, beaming brightly to right and left. 'I'll get my geological expert through here. The full shipment will arrive next month. Good day, sir. Look sharp you boys, as I guess you want a drink afore we ride to the creek.'

Waving his cigar, genially urging forward his four boys, who appeared to be carrying twice as many saddle-bags and gunny-sacks as when they entered, and all twice as heavy, the big easterner swept through the small gate and headed for the door.

'Good luck, Mister Crater!' sang out Hank Williams, receiving a cigar from the great man, which he boastfully waved to the other clerks as he escorted the entire company outside.

It was in a manner oddly stiff and slow and akin to a burial ceremony, that the Bruce Gang passed outside into main street. Then at once they noticed it – there was definitely something wrong, something uncanny and forbidding in the air. The heat met them and seemed to wrap choking claws around their throats. The brilliant sunshine had become a sickly yellow light, playing deceptively with one's eyesight. The two groups of horses, one outside the best saloon and the other outside the general store, had been gradually herded forward by two sets of lookouts. The mounts came opposite the bank steps at the exact moment they were required. On the bottom step sat two kids in bare feet and shirts, glumly staring at a now empty jar. Except for these urchins the town was deserted, silent and gloomy as an open grave, just as if some terrible disaster impended. Stealthily the gang came down the steps, deliberately retarding their movements, which increased the interior torture of suspense. It was like walking along a razor's edge, as Rand anxiously mused, bringing up the rear of the party. At each downward step they expected either shouts of alarm from behind, or a shattering volley from the front. Nothing happened, however. The kids gawked at them, drinking in every detail, enviously watched them mount up, and sighingly watched them plod away in a manner admirably lazy and carefree. The Bruce Gang headed out of Flintstone.

'Storm a-brewing,' Hank Williams tremulously whispered, having leapt up behind Rand. 'Think we'll make the desert?'

Rand did not reply. Hank leaned away to look at him, and anxiously wet and rolled the unlit cigar in his lips. Rand's face was as chill, expressionless and dead as a marble plaque.

Slowly and watchfully the men rode down the street. Nothing stirred. A baby was still howling in a shack somewhere to the right. A thirsty tinkling of water could be distinctly heard long before they thudded across the bridge over the creek. Gunfire was expected to explode that sinister silence at any moment: yet it did not come. The buildings thinned out, concluded with a saw-mill, then came a few ragged tents draped with ragged washing, then an area of pot-holes, abandoned diggings, broken and rusted picks and shovels, heaps of rubbish, and finally a bush-strewn plain, stretching in a fever of sickness beneath the queer sun. They were outside Flintstone, and still safe. The gang began to trot, to gallop, and soon raced along at a tempestuous pace, while the town dwindled into a haze of deep silence, and the horizon ahead began to grow that thankful line of little hills which introduced the running desert.

The rushing air, the quick action and releasing of strained senses brought an exhilarating relief. When finally reaching a trail which wound between the little hills, the raiders slowed down. Many and anxious had been their backward glances as the miles passed by, though now those glances had turned upon the stupendous loads of wealth slung across the four leading horses. The sight of such bulging bags of dollar bills was mighty encheering; they feasted their eyes greedily; they became intoxicated by the spirit of success. They shouted, laughed, praised one another, and joked over the more excit-ing particulars of their robbery. They had waited a long, long time for this moment, and they meant to squeeze every drop of satisfaction from every detail, come what may. They drew rein at Sulphur Springs.

Stretching before them was the desert, a spectacle real awe-inspiring under the drunken-eyed sun: that sun was filling every man with a half-recognized feeling of uneasiness. Behind them, racing in silent pursuit, gorging earth and sky and fear-ful to behold, came a mighty wall of grey dust, all thick and billowing and pierced by vicious streaks of crackling fire.

'Hell's a-coming!' shouted Bruce, his horse prancing round the water-hole. 'Best get all the water you can carry, boys.'

'Will you chance it?' queried Rand, solemnly jerking a thumb behind him.

'You bet,' laughed Bruce. 'It will cover our tracks in fine style; you'll see. We divide here, Symes, splitting everything evenly. We'll meet at Sweetwater. Just keep to the desert, and devil take the storm.'

'Nothing suits me better,' shouted Symes, leering wickedly as he personally took charge of a loaded pair of saddle-bags. 'I'll see you sitting pretty in old Sweetwater.'

'Say, but wasn't it a smooth thing? Never knowed a bank hold-up work so slick,' chuckled Tom. 'Why, I had more trouble getting apples when I was a kid. Did you see that cashier's face, though? He just yanked open yon office door, then goggled like he was a derned fish on a hook.'

A great roar of mirth revealed everybody's appreciation; yes, even Tom's jokes were side-splitters now.

'Fish on a hook nothing,' argued Mex, whose laughter made speaking difficult for him, 'Jeengo, but that fella died sudden! He gasped like a flattened toad.'

'Cleanest bank job I ever took a hand in.' Hank Williams chuckled, trying to look modest under Mex's praise. 'A straight million dollars, I wager. You know what? I'm a-going to live in cool luxury. Damn me! What a pay-off!'

They heard a strange hiss. Hank heard nothing, however: a bullet was boring through the back of his skull and entering his brain.

CHAPTER TWELVE

There came a mighty explosion of guns. What with the storm a-brewing real bad, it seemed like an earthquake.

Hank Williams slid lifeless from behind Rand. Other riders, with their mounts rearing and whining, cursed and tumbled before the tempest of lead. Then Tom and Larry began to return the fire, and were soon joined by the barking guns of Symes and Rand, who hazily recognized, in the churning dust and sinister light, a ruthless line of bushwhackers behind the little hills on either side of Sulphur Springs.

Totally unprepared for a gun-battle at this late stage in the big venture, and being in a rejoicing frame of mind, it clashed upon the Bruce Gang with a tremendous shock, throwing them into devastating confusion, and threatening them with a massacre.

Jake was second to die; he died in the saddle, his horse running wild, carrying the limp body into the desert to God knows where. The horses kept milling in a frenzy round the water-hole, some threshed on their backs in the cacti thickets, staining the thorny vegetation with their blood. Mercilessly the guns thundered, pouring a continuous stream of lead into the mass of living flesh. Then, Tom, poor Tom lay screaming like a kid, clutching his saddle-bags from which fluttered a trail of bullet-pierced dollar bills. Now other men were crawling away through the sand, dragging themselves on their elbows, swearing, moaning, yelling, wildly blasting their weapons at those death-spitting hills. To stay and fight would be suicide; to break away would need a miracle; yet Rand suddenly glimpsed a free passage into the desert. He was about to dig spurs into his horse when Clemens, the old-timer with the tapering beard, the fellow who was a-going to do something mysteriously special with his share-out, cried his name.

Rand swirled around: Clemens was floundering for his life in the pool; Rand was about to assist him. At that instant Mister Sturdy's horse reared, creased by a bullet, crazy in pain: its hoofs crushed into the old man's appealing face. Jeff Rand's heart shook in horror.

It was growing darker. Some awesome change was coming over the world.

The flashing and pounding of guns as the gang retaliated in blind fury, the breath-catching whine of bullets, and the colliding and wrestling of man and beast, grew worse. The enemy lay hidden; he could not be sought out; nobody tried to identify him; everybody just kept madly seeking escape from that orderly repetition of gunfire. Big Bruce shouted like a man insane, shouted commands that no one understood, that no one could obey if they had understood. A few moments ago when he had looked back, seen the storm blowing up, and told Rand hell was a-coming, he had not known the truth of his words. It was here, ravaging them with all its satanic forces. The whole dreadful tumult, beginning at close quarters, suggested some devilish machine, grinding faster and fiercer, not solely bent on wiping out the Bruce Gang, but on bursting to pieces the whole mad world.

'Ride!' Rand began yelling, holstering his weapons and charging round in circles. 'Make a break, boys! Into the desert; follow me! Ride, you blasting half-wits! Ride!'

The darkness had greatly increased. The heavens were growling queerly. The earth was beginning to lift itself in a hissing river of sand. The desert was on the run.

Rand dug spurs into his animal, and with what appeared to be a standing leap, he cleared the water-hole and the old-timer's poor body. He ran with the sand. He fancied other figures imitating his example. At that moment the storm engulfed the scene.

Overhead the howling dropped lower, wilder, sucking up the sand in great spinning columns. Within a few more seconds everything was on the move, and the unreal night was transformed into a hideous inferno of choking filth and blinding flashes. The water, the rocks and cacti and ghostly balls of tumbleweed, even the dead bodies, as well as wounded men and horses, all started to drift before the unseen power. Still the enemy guns kept pounding flashing and barking with redoubled force, seemingly more enraged to find the confused remnant of the gang being preserved from a massacre, being driven after that streaking form of horse and rider, which was Rand.

The chase began, but the chase was brief. Only once did the raiders catch a glimpse of their attackers, of a furiously yelling and shooting company of miners, more than fifty-strong, thirsting for blood and in hot pursuit. Then the flying sand obliterated the view of that surging horde which chilled one's heart. Gradually the shooting subsided, swallowed up by the more giddying roar of the storm. Even so one still kept fancying shots and shouts, imagining chasing figures, sensing whistling lead, coming from   all directions for long afterwards. Time passed. The wind had developed. The riders felt as though they straddled winged beasts, whose hoofs noiselessly flayed the air, whose sides panted like noiseless bellows, and whose destination was some mysterious place in a lost and wasted world.

Sand, white and fine as snow, yet dry and hot as cinders; sand that blinded and deafened and gritted between one's teeth, driving men crazy. Killer sand which had turned this one-time luxurious cattle-country into a plain of the nether regions, ultimately breaking the hearts of the old pioneers.

How long the miserably reduced Bruce Gang had been riding, they could not tell. Their pockets and shirt-fronts were a-bulge with tight-packed grit; the nostrils of their beasts were caked over. Each animal now quivering and floundering between each rider's legs, was ready to run wild or drop dead. Rand ruthlessly led them onward; through belly-deep drifts his own mount gamely struggled, haunting him with a fear of a broken leg, for without a horse a man would be wrestling hopelessly in the arms of death.

A rift in the storm momentarily exposed a feverish yellow light streaked with red, like an indian's war-paint: it was close on sundown. Several hours had therefore passed in delirium since the ambush at Sulphur Springs, all without a halt, without a word, and in the dread of another sudden gunbattle from that army of Flintstone miners. Some of the men were wounded, one was dying, and every fellow was baffled, scared and cringing in the pressure of thirst. Six men had died back there, two had wandered away in the storm, half the booty, about half a million dollars had been lost, and now in this merciless desert they had lost themselves.

It was Rand who eventually led them into comparative shelter between howling dunes, rising like canyon walls; and thus, never realising it, Rand made the greatest mistake of his life.

The men dismounted and drank from half-empty flasks, screwed dust from eyes and ears and began to breathe and think again. They regarded with sullen and distrustful looks the remaining saddle-bags of dollars. Fear and anxiety became submerged in a rising anger. Each man's selfish thought made him hostile and wary of his neighbour.

Big Bruce panted and wrathfully beat the sand from his clothing as he crossed over to the lone rider, who was washing his horses nostrils. For the past couple of hours one vital question had rankled in Bruce's brain, and now feelings erupted.

'Rand! Who runs this outfit, you or me?' he exploded in a dry and barking voice. 'Who gives orders?'

'Who tipped off the sheriff of Flintstone? There's the real question.' Symes roared above the wind, as he stood with feet astride and hands on his hips, facing Rand and all of them. 'Someone here thinks he's smart, and I aim to find him if I kills everybody in the derned process. Who is the dirty spy?'

'Yeah, that's right. Who done it?' the men echoed in fierce chorus, clearly afraid of being singly accused by Symes, and all sending suspicious glances to Rand.

'That sheriff knowed we was busting his bank.' Big Bruce snarled in uncontrollable rage, his attention on Rand who completely ignored him. 'That sheriff had a posse of a hundred diggers; leastways fifty, all prepared, anticipating our moves, knowing we'd stop for water at the spring. What's the opinion of our new leader, Mister Rand?'

'Lucky for us the storm blew in, otherwise it would have been a clean sweep for the sheriff,' mused Mister Sturdy.

'Why, it's wuss than murder!' somebody shouted in rising passion. 'Think of that old man, what never hurt nobody.'

'Some lousy sidewinder here has double-dealt his buddies,' Symes repeated venemously. 'Look sharp and sort him out, boys, or there's the devil to pay, and that's me.'

'Mebbe we don't have to search far,' shouted Bruce, who did not try to conceal his suspicion at all. 'We men have operated together for a long time. We know each other pretty well. There's only one queer new-comer in this outfit. Well, Rand, what do you say?'

Symes grunted and looked displeased, fell thoughtful for a few seconds, then suddenly raised his head, laughing hideously. The men started to close in around Jeff.

'Wait!' Mister Sturdy leapt up the side of the dune behind Rand and raised his arms in a peace-appealing manner. 'Just a moment, boys. We have no time for a lynching. Sure we've lost half our men, but shareouts will remedy that. First, let's quit this infernal desert, if we can, then let's sort out the culprit at Sweetwater, hold trial in fine style, and satisfy ourselves with a hanging.'

'That's a load o' ballyhoo! I allow you're a clever schemer, Mister Sturdy,' confessed Bruce, balling his fists, 'and if it weren't for you we wouldn't be rich men today. But keep your hand out of this affair. We don't need no trial.'

'Naturally not. We know who killed the Crocker boys to begin with,' growled Shorty.

'We know who stirred poison from the start, and who disappeared queerly when we hit town,' pointed out Mex, looking murderously at Rand retying a small parcel to his saddle.

'Rand called at the hardware store, that's all,' said Sturdy. 'He was only buying some leather to patch his saddle.'

'So that was his excuse. Did you fellas know the hardware store is next to the sheriff's office? You paid the sheriff a private call, didn't you, Rand?' Bruce drew closer. 'Never mind, you don't have to speak; you don't need to do a thing, Mister. We'll soon straighten things out for our murdering squealer. Mebbe the sheriff was a-going to pay you well, clear your record, give you a new start, huh?'

Symes' humour expanded into insane guffaws; apparently he discovered something uncommonly funny in the last remark.

'Rand!' Bruce screamed in his rage, as he crouched there

like some awful human monster in the flowing tide of sand. 'Rand my buck, you always roused fire in my innards, but now you've kindled a blasting furnace. I'm a-going to rip yuh bone from bone, yeah, with my bare hands. Take his guns, Symes!' He ended with a vicious command.

At that Jeff spun around, tensed for speedy action. Blearily he looked over Bruce's massive frame.

'Bet I get four o' you lousy rats afore I check out,' he wagered. 'Come on. Try your bone-dissecting, big mouth, and you'll be first to die.'

Such was the confidence of his steadily delivered threat, as to repel them at once. Dismay twisted Bruce's face, while the other men fell motionless but nonetheless hostile.

'Get him, Symes!' the boss yelled again in a frenzy. 'You're the gunfighter in this outfit. Get him! It's an order. I didn't hire you to stand laughing like a jackass. Kill him, Symes!'

Long and solemn became the face of Mister Symes as he regarded first the furious boss, and next the taut figure of that wild beast, Rand.

'Sorry about this, Jeff,' sympathised Symes, making a preparatory act of hooking his thumbs in his belt, just as he behaved before poor Merrick died. 'Why is it that every fella I fancy, does a dirty trick and get himself under my guns?'

'Kill him, Symes!' Bruce kept panting ferociously, drinking in the scene with wicked pleasure.

The men edged away, fearful alarm on their faces. Rand faced the killer.

Not for one second did Jeff believe he could beat Bruce in fistwork – yet the possibility of beating Symes in gun-draw, well, it was sheerly ridiculous! But there was no way out; death trapped him; and this agony of waiting would not be prolonged, not under these circumstances. There would be no long torture as Smily had suffered in the gulch. Symes was ready to force forward the gunfight.

'Drop your belt!'

Rand felt guns prodding into his back. Sturdy's voice arose from behind him. A fresh anticipative growling passed among the men; they might yet have personal satisfaction. Rand hesitated, heard the command a second time, and slowly complied, his mind working rapidly though uselessly. Mister Sturdy picked up his guns with the greatest care imaginable, as if he moved in the vicinity of some unsafe load of gunpowder; and he also led away Rand's horse.

'Aw, that was a dirty trick!' objected Symes, looking mournful. 'I no sooner get me a job and some other fella swipes it. If this goes on it will give me a bad temper, and ruin my gentle nature completely.'

'Never mind, Symes. This should be real live entertainment,' prophesied Bruce, leering at his now helpless prey as he unfastened his own gunbelt. 'I've dreamt of this day. Let me catch him without them guns. That's what I kept saying to myself. Stand back, you boys!'

'Come out the way, fellas. Let Bruce in at him,' urged Mex, grinning and twisting his own large fists together.

'I ain't ever seen a body ripped bone from bone,' Symes mused loudly. 'You know what? I feel like a kid at his first sideshow. I can hardly wait. Go at him, Bruce!'

Capable as Bruce was with his fists, and with a long history of experiences behind him, he now swept his shirt from his brawny body and attacked Rand over-eagerly. One second Rand was standing limply and sadly awaiting the punishment, yet next moment he had sprung into energetic action. Drawing back both fists at waist-level, he lunged for the boss's middle. Shock, pain, fury, recorded themselves on the big man's face. He staggered back, panting and turning blue, wheezing and sucking in the flying sand.

'Bone from bone, remember,' drawled Symes, biting his thumbnail ruminatively. 'Lordy, lordy me! Just whose skeleton was you meaning, Brucy-boy?' he added with a disdainful chuckle. 'Guess I had best use my guns after all.'

'Shut up! You just wait. I'll fix the varmint. You'll see.' Bruce, raving madly, regained his balance and his wind, and began to circle like a coyote. 'Watch this, Symes! See me maul this gun-grabber so's he never – never draws irons agin.' He came nearer. 'Rand! I'm a-going to smash your hands to little bits!'

Here was Jeff Rand's foremost dread: damaged hands. Nothing else Bruce might have said could have struck home with real fear: it sent a shudder through Rand, who had spent most of his life avoiding certain tasks and physical violence to preserve his life-guarding hands. Now, during the succeeding moments Big Bruce sought to carry out his threat, filling Rand with frenzied action. The boss attacked shrewdly, forcefully, using tricks totally foreign to his opponent. There was little Jeff could manage to do against the pounding onslaught, except keep backing away and trying to hide his face and those precious hands. Yet soon his face and ears were bleeding profusely, while an agony of breathing implied that his ribs were being broken apart. He never struck another blow: he felt his fingers bruised at every joint; but it was not serious, not yet; back, back, back he floundered up the side of the dune. He tried to use his feet on the great monster's head, but Bruce wrenched at his ankles and hauled him down in the tons of flowing sand. It was with a continuous stream of threats and foul-mouthed remarks that Bruce worked, brutally worked, seeking to beat and break Rand's body. Nothing save a miracle could rescue Rand from being pounded to death.

Due to his retreating and unresisting behaviour, the whole onset became delightfully easy to the boss. Over-confidence, deliberately played for by Rand, soon returned to Big Bruce, helped by the bellowed admiration of the men who milled around them. The penalty came of a sudden. Unexpected energy returned to Jeff, when down again came both his fists; and once again, this time with all the strength of his long and flexible body, he rammed the same double blow into the big man's stomach. Bruce stiffened, released a beast-like howl, and collapsed.

Rand nevertheless understood that, at precisely this time, he had reached his limit. If Bruce came again it would be final.

Believing their leader to be beaten, the mounting emotions of the men rose to a climax. Fiercely and collectively they fell upon Rand whose wild-cat opposition was just wasted power.

'Break his fingers! Crush his hands! Kill him, boys!'

Bruce – he was up again; he was shrieking like a maniac, pained, humiliated, flaming with uncontrollable wrath. Nothing but an axe seemed powerful enough to lay low that great mad bull of a man. Groggily he charged into the struggling mass of men, bent on assisting the end of the slaughter.

Symes was laughing. Symes was laughing hideously and shrilly, and rocking to and fro, and clenching at his belt till veins stood out on his well-kept hands. He sounded and acted like a son of the devil.

Had the Bruce Gang forsaken its senses? Had the long ordeal of tensed waiting at the gulch, the nerve-straining robbery, and the ultimate tragedy frayed and snapped the chords of commonsense, turning men into beasts? Or was there something in this ruthless desert that imparted strange savagery, that stirred some primal instinct in the breast of man? All the fellows, seeming to forget they were human-beings, ferociously struggled over their single enemy, madly thirsted for Rand's blood. Blood alone would satisfy and when they saw it fresh hatred impassioned them. With bare hands they sought to destroy; and then with rocks they sought to

111

crush Rand's broken hands.

Round that scene of violence swirled the desert, being lifted and hurled in dense clouds by a yet mightier wind, whose howling ascended to a screach upon the dune-tops. The storm attuned itself to the hellish spectacle, incensed it – then, unexpectedly, offered a chance of escape and refuge to the half-dead victim.

The sand dune started to slide. It became a rapidly flowing river, in which each man grew desperate to preserve his own life. They began to swim down it; and a strangled scream, as one of them was smothered and lost forever, forced home the grim death confronting everybody. Exactly what occurred, or under what circumstances Jeff Rand managed to reach the desert floor and tumble clear, was all too confused to relate. He thought he heard Mister Sturdy screaming in his ear. Somehow he found his guns and belt slung around his neck. A moment afterwards he was clinging giddily to the back of his leaping animal. The feel, the smell of its soft hide was down-right affectionate, real soothing, and he was riding, stumbling, tearing away. God be thanked! He was free. He was alone.

'Ride, Jeff m'lad! Ride, son, or die!' He kept hearing Mister Sturdy's voice. Suddenly the voice altered its tone. 'This way, Bruce! There he goes!'

The shooting began; and it had almost died away into the roaring of the storm when, convulsing the limp body sprawled along the speeding horse, a bullet tore into Rand. He was done.

The wind moaned dismally. The animal swerved and whinnied pathetically, its master's blood coursing down its neck. Sand swept above and below; and into the full blast of it the horse bravely battled of its own accord. Darkness was closing in like oblivion.

CHAPTER THIRTEEN

Dawn slanted across the desert, and the desert was hushed, its sand was motionless, ribbed like a seashore, and just as grey as that dawn. A prevalent air of waiting spread itself across the world, while in the distance receded an awesome wall of blackness, contrasting greatly with the green shoreline of the desert in the opposite direction. Towards this shoreline of weeds and rocks travelled a lone rider, lurching oddly in the saddle, and never once raising his head to scan the desolate expanse of land. His horse plodded at random, sometimes halting to sample bunches of crisp weed, and sometimes snorting and running from crawling creatures that began to scurry back and forth over the sandy ribs. This was the outer edge of the running desert.

At first little breezy disturbances lay in the wake of the storm, though these soon dwindled away: gradually the air acquired a quality of stillness that was strangely perfect. It became difficult to breathe. The sunrise was a long time coming; certainly it needed a break after stewing such a course of hot days, yet it had no call to hang-fire altogether. Even the grey light already spread around was losing itself. Great herds of cloud were stampeding across the sky. Nearer and nearer the solitary rider came drifting to the desert's rim,

113

seemingly heading from nowhere into nowhere. Then, with shocking suddenness, a tumbling of thunder rocked the world. The crawling creatures out yonder ceased to scutter, crouched, tensed, alert, more keenly waiting. The horse had leapt and whinnied, and now, with a wild shaking of its body, it broke into a smart canter. The rider had not stirred.

At once large drops like dollar pieces started to fall upon the earth: little balls of dust began to swarm everywhere like an invasion of funny little bugs. The earth murmured back at the skies in a prayer of thanksgiving; a merry hiss arose from the brown weeds; a far-away mesquite bush rocked and twittered; the crawling creatures darted around with revived life, held out their tongues, rolled over, showed their hot bellies to the rain, and set up a pleasant chirruping and croaking. Sure enough all things were downright glad, and all slaked their burning thirst, all except that single rider. He gave no attention; he just rocked to and fro in the saddle, leaving his horse to climb across the craggy desert edge, and to head for the refreshing prairies released by the running sand.

Hours soaked away. The horse sludged across mud-flats, reached a great expanse of considerably decent rangeland, and eventually came upon a trail winding through Grasshopper Valley. After following the trail for a while the animal pricked forward its ears; a few seconds later the rattling of a wagon could be heard distinctly. Then swerving reckessly round a bend, came a ramshackle buckboard driven by an old cowhand who yelled, chewed and spat to left and right with machine-like regularity. The mud was flying, the rain was blinding, and the old fellow's naturally watery vision prevented him from seeing anything clearly ahead of him. Thus it was only at the point of being trodden down and churned under wheels that the lone rider halted, stiffly drawing himself upright in the saddle. The buckboard sliddered to a standstill, and as he stared at it he instinctively reached for a gun. A searing pain at once arrested his movement.

'Don't try it, Mister young fella!' shouted the buckboard driver, his horny hands suddenly jerking up a shotgun. 'Another toughnut, huh? Hostile, too, it seems. I jest cain't figure what this district's a-coming to, with mad hellions lurking almost everywheres. Gold sure is a curse.'

'Where – where am I, neighbour?'

'Pretty obvious, ain't it?'snapped the oldster, cocking his weapon and blowing beads of rain from his drooping moustache. 'You're on my range and under my sights.'

'What? What's this? More – more gunfighting?'

The strained words trailed away. Jeff Rand tumbled out of the saddle.

'Holy smoke! Guess I must look derned tough, despite what Ma sez!' exclaimed the old rancher.

The horse began to nose the blood-smeared and senseless heap of misery that sprawled in the mud.

The driver climbed down for a closer inspection, holding his shotgun ready.

'Holy smoke!' he repeated with mounting intelligence and horror. 'Say, what a gruesome sight! Looks like he was scalped, wearing his face battered in that way.' He bent down and loosened Rand's waistcoat, thereat making discoveries which provoked more profane language. 'Ribs bust – bullet in shoulder, and . . .' The old man's searching gaze finally alighted on Jeff's hands, and despite himself he gulped in a gush of pity. 'Dern it; the fella has been mauled real bad! Whoever did that to another man's hands – well! – he needs burning. Lift up, neighbour. Steady now; I'll take yuh home to Ma. Shucks, hoss, quit nosing me that way; your boss ain't dead!'

Within a few moments the buckboard had turned in the trail and rattled back round the bend at a steadier rate, carrying Rand and pursued by the weary horse. The twin ruts left behind quickly filled and overflowed. The first stream for many years was born in Grasshopper Valley. One could hardly believe the desert had one-time smothered the land.

Sunshine streamed like vapourised gold through the ranch-house window. Sweet odour came from the knotted plank walls. Jeff Rand first grew aware of the light, then the soothing warmth, and next the pleasant mingling of pinewood and baking cookies. Gradually as he recovered his senses responded to a number of altered, unexpected and confusing things. For instance he was in a bed, a real bed, not a sleeping bag or a bunk; furthermore there were cool and affectionate sheets around him; not a hairy horse-blanket but parchment-like sheets that rasped against a fellow's chin right queerly. Next thing he noticed was a dreamy lowing of cattle, a buzzing of insects, and a real homely clink of cooking utensils. Peaceful! Why, it was so peaceful, refined and removed from the coarse things he was accustomed to having around, that it got him scared quite a piece at first. His own ranching days were awakened in his memory. Say, supposing he looked out of yonder window, would he see Pa out there on the range? Or supposing he opened that cream coloured door, would he hear his sister Jenny singing?

When gold was found in forty-eight, the people said 'twas gas,
And some were fools enough to think the lumps were only brass!

Rand, drowsy-headed, tried to grin at his thoughts, but his face had a peculiar hurting stiffness. So, raising his hands to find what the trouble could be, he received a terrible shock.

With stupefied eyes he stared at the splints and glove-like bandages covering those hands – his gun hands – both of them – each afire inside and bleeding and ruined. Oh lord! From now on he was just – just a dead man!

Recollection flowed back swiftly and with frightening reality. He remembered first the gold mine and the murder of Jim Miller. Then came the long riding – gunfights – Bruce Gang – bank robbery – ambush – sandstorm – and finally, hell! A hell ringing to the fiendish laughter of Symes. Symes the killer, inhumanly rapid, and the only man who filled Rand with a shaking dread. As Jeff lay there his eyes brightened in fear. Of a sudden he started to search around for his guns, under the soft pillows, the sheets, and on the side table. Symes might pay a call; he must get ready, must find those guns. But, oh lord, these hands!

Moaning deliriously Rand fell to biting and ripping the bandages.

'Where you looking for these?'

He heard it; a low voice coming from a far shadowy corner. No, it wasn't Symes; it sounded mild and gentle like a woman's voice. Feverishly Rand strained to sit upright, and his gaze travelled from the old shot-gun on the wall to the hanging oil-lamp, from the chairs with old-fashioned twisted limbs to a cattleman's calendar. The calendar advertised grain, and stunned Rand with the date it showed. It was Monday. Somewhere he had lost three days.

'Don't remove those bandages, please, or you might never use your hands agin, nor these things.'

Oh, yes, the voice; he had nearly forgotten about it. He must be losing his senses to forget a thing like that. Struggling over to his right side he saw her; she was sitting in a stream of sunlight; she was young and plainly dressed; she was nimbly darting needle and cotton in and out of a shirt – his shirt.

117

Beside her on a table were a newly-oiled pair of six-guns – his guns!

'Who the blazes are you? And where the blazes am I?'

'Who the blazes wants to know?' she gently inquired, snapping the thread with her teeth and inspecting various other parts of the frayed garment. 'Never mind, you need not answer my question, neighbour, because you ain't to talk much. Ma's word is law round here. I'm her niece. You're on the Keller spread.'

It took a long time for this information to register, and when he finally managed it Rand was unable to find a sensible reply, so he just said:

'Aw! Where's my hoss?'

'Ma don't allow them in the bedrooms,' she replied, very secretively. 'They breathe too heavy.'

'Yes, ma'am,' murmured Jeff, very serious and real subdued, not at all seeing her fun-making in his dazed state. 'Is it all right to smoke, ma'am?'

'That depends, neighbour. Just mind them sheets, that's all. Here, mebbe I had better twist up the 'baccy for you,' she whispered in a voice that grew husky as she remembered the state of his hands. 'I have only one thing to warn you of, Mister Rand. Ma and Pa Keller are out-and-out gentlefolk, what don't read the chronicle as I do. Understand? Then I would be obliged if, while you're on this ranch, you kept quiet about your gunfighting experiences. Here's your smoke.'

'Thanks, ma'am,' murmured Jeff, feeling even more subdued, with his mind busily recognizing the charity of these poor folk. 'It seems I'm deep indebted to the old couple.'

'You are,' she promptly replied, attacking the collar of the shirt with a rapidly flicking needle. 'And so am I.'

A long pause followed, during which Rand reflectively studied her while she kept sending distrustful glances to that pair of black six-guns.

'You look awful like my sister did,' Jeff feverishly declared.

'Many young women look awful, neighbour,' she calmly answered him.

'Sure, ma'am. That is to say – I mean – oh, no! You see, my sister is dead.'

'Oh!' She glanced up quickly. 'I am all sympathy for your sis, neighbour, and your comparison is a real honour.' She smiled, raising an eyebrow up and down, looking very cute.

Rand became restless; he felt hot; his temperature was up pretty bad just then. He nevertheless smiled, sighed heavily, and closing his eyes he quietly said:

'Jest like Jenny, anyhow. Jest like home. Mebbe it ain't good riding alone all along the way.'

Another lengthy interlude of silence occurred. Beginning to look fretful once more, Rand strove again to sit upright.

'Begging your pardon, ma'am, but did any strangers call, asking for me? Did you see a gay-dressed, dark-skinned rider, wearing an uncommonly broad gunbelt?'

'No, Mister Rand. Nobody's bin out here since Lew fetched in the mail two days gone, and brought the shocking news of Flintstone bank-robbery.' Her hands ceased to work as she watched him intently. Her information only seemed to weary him. 'We all are naturally curious to know what befell yuh, neighbour, though you won't be finding us prying into your affairs none,' she went on, rising to leave, and casting a parting glance at the black six-guns. 'The less we know the less worry for us all, perhaps. Personally I don't think you're a killer, are you? Maybe you didn't rob that bank, did you?' She waited unrewarded for answers, then, smiling she said: 'Rest easy, Mister Rand. I'll go tell Ma you're awake and hollerin' for grub.'

Jeff returned her smile as she closed the door, and released a deeper sigh, aware of a rare peace.

That awakening at the Keller homestead was the commencement of a spell of happy content for the cruelly injured drifter. The kindly company and attentions of the old folk were indescribably grand to Jeff; he had forgotten such people really existed, and he was inclined to reverence them with awe as lofty holy ones. It made him feel a right down sinful creature at first, until he got to know them better; not that he found them less decent as time passed or anything like that, but they just got around to making a fellow feel at home with them and himself. Nonetheless Jeff was kind of glad to find the old man could curse like pitch when he warmed up, which went a long way to making the place more bearable and human-like in Jeff's eyes. Sure he was grateful, although he felt caged up and awkward for a time, and downright reluctant to surrender his independence. For the first few days he yearned to run away, hideout someplace in the wastelands, and nurse his own wounds himself like a wild animal. That was specially because Pa had to dress him, because Ma had to wash him, right down to the neck-line, and because Teresa had to feed him like a kid, roll his smokes and perform many other like things. That, for an independent saddle-tramp such as Rand, was humiliation in the raw. One thing struck him as odd, and began to frighten him: nobody ever rebandaged or even mentioned his hands.

Anyhow, life went along extra-good, and the sinner-among-saints feeling declined, while Ma set about straightening out some of his grief-twisted opinions. Of course there were drawbacks to the situation, drawbacks he knew he would never bear for long. For instance, a fellow couldn't chew 'baccy in bed; and when the wounds got to throbbing pretty bad, he just couldn't relieve his feelings with red-hot language when the ladies were present. Naturally he had tried it, and the shock was sort of stunning for everybody concerned, even for Rand. Getting more familiar in this fashion, Jeff started gentle inquiries to Ma about his hands, but she behaved so motherly in response, and left the room with such a dose of hay-fever, when there wasn't a whisp of the stuff on the poverty-stricken place, that Jeff Rand began seriously to believe the worst. His gunfighting days were at an end.

Ma Keller was a fine old lady; she kept quiet most times, but she was the ruler. She allowed Pa pretend he was governor, and that pleased Pa, except when things got tangled and his temper boiled over, then Ma straightened him out good and plenty. Rand liked the old woman; and sometimes when a motherly smile creased her trouble-hardened face, Rand knew she was specially sacred. It certainly made him feel comfortable, her taking his presence quite natural that way. The old man, however, was the prying and talkative type, dangerous without knowing it. He was not tall and bony and elegant like Ma, but thick-set and nowheres near so brainy neither. Pa made Jeff uneasy; Pa was curious, naturally, and eager to acquaint himself with Jeff's affairs. When that happened, as Jeff rightly mused, there would be real trouble. The sheriff of Flintstone would then be organising a hanging, and Rand would be supplying the neck.

'Seen any strangers out riding today, Miss Teresa?'

'No, Mister Rand. There ain't no gold on the Keller range.'

This confidential and anxious piece of conversation took place without a miss. It became like a kind of ritual between them. Although Teresa concealed it, she felt somewhat honoured to be acting as Rand's lookout. She faithfully kept secret her knowledge of his identity, yet she both distrusted him and pitied him, which to Rand was an interesting combination. Another thing, she was a poor hand with a razor even for a girl, and Jeff decided to dispense with her, leaving Pa just

121

to take the top layer of skin off with his rough-shod methods, and a razor like a scythe. Teresa was an all-round nuisance – mainly because her cheery visits were so brief.

But, as Jeff Rand's situation grew more pleasant, so grew a dread of endangering these simple honest folk. He was only deceiving them and himself by staying at the ranch: he was no harmless drifting cowpoke set upon by thieves; no, he was a slick gunfighter, a dealer in death, a bank robber and a wanted man. Thus his presence incriminated these people, threatened them with a raid from the Bruce Gang who could not now afford to leave him alive. Above all their lives became similarly threatened by the ruthless guns of killer Symes.

Many times Rand made private attempts to arise and leave when these fears afflicted him. But he was still too weak. Yet he must get away somehow, for the days were passing alarmingly quick. He must operate his plan before it was too late. His hands, however – what could a fellow do with such hands? Just how bad were they? They felt dead.

Every kindness Rand now received at the Keller ranch added to his bitter torment. Every drop of happiness was fast absorbed in miserably burning impatience. Beneath Rand's calm exterior burned a desperate hell.

CHAPTER FOURTEEN

Fear prevented Rand from uncovering his hands. Day by day the fear developed in him, keeping him obedient to Ma Keller's wishes; until the morning arrived when he was allowed downstairs. Thereafter his manner became disturbingly strange to the Keller folk.

It was early morning. He had just become freighted with breakfast, and now he sat rocking it back and forth and picking his teeth, enjoying the smoothly running comfort of Pa's rocker on the veranda. A faint pinkness was spreading over the sky, and he could see for miles across the range, with its reef-like ridges of sand, and its dismally few head of cattle, rawboned, wild as buffalo, and bawling restlessly as they searched for a meal in patches of tough bunch-grass.

'Old man Keller, the great cattle king,' mused Rand. 'Keller, the only fella what fought the running desert and lived. A plum stubborn old cuss. He shoulda pulled up his stakes and freighted his folk and cattle same as everybody else did when the dry winds came. There was just one other man with that fighting pioneer spirit, and that was Jim Miller. I like him.'

The comparison, however, introduced a new and infuriating train of thought. Rand rocked back and forth more heatedly, his gaze fastened on the now burning sky.

'Jim Miller's gold, found and lost,' he almost muttered aloud. 'Somewhere out yonder is the cold-blooded killer, hiding out with the Bruce Gang. I wonder whereabouts is that place Sweetwater.'

The rocker began to rattle and creak under the heavier motion, and, edging back a few inches, started to thud against the log wall. If Rand noticed it he did not care in his angrily abstracted frame of mind; but the Keller folk found it somewhat nerve-racking. Pa did not like it one bit, because it upset his digestion, and he carried a load of affection for his rocker and his ranch-house wall. They began to watch the culprit through the window.

'Must get these hands straight – I must!' they heard Rand mutter fiercely. 'Supposing Jim's killer was really Sturdy? Ordinarily I would stand a chance agin him, but now I can't even practise up just in case. Holy smoke, it gives me a kind of sinking sickness thinking of it!' Rand raised his covered hands before him and sucked deeply at the chill morning air. 'It's no good feeling like a scared kid. There ain't a chance of playing hookey with this deal. Never trust myself agin if I did that. If I run away just once, then I will really grow affeared – yeah, and soon get myself plugged by a gun-proud squirt like the Crockers.'

A resounding thud ended the rhythm of the old rocker. The Kellers looked shocked at each other. Rand had reached a firm decision and, trembling and with moisture standing out on his brow, he was now tearing frantically with his teeth at the bandages. It was a frightening sight to see; it was like watching the actions of some trapped wild animal, scared into unbelievable ferocity, ready to tear the heart out of any living thing that dared to cause an obstruction. At that moment the old folk knew they sheltered a dangerous man, a man apparently

124

haunted and impassioned by a life of bloodshed.

Pa and Ma and Teresa stood tensed and silent, pale and strained, captured by strange fascination as they witnessed the tearing away of the blood-stained rags. Rand's long pent up impatience released itself more and more as he progressed without interruption from anybody. How he had waited for and dreaded this moment! Sure he had felt queer movements and stabbing pains inside these bandages for a few days now, and he was fully prepared for the worst of expectations to be realised. He cursed aloud; he didn't care any more; and with a series of unwindings and rippings the bandages came off. A dead silence followed, a silence fraught with horror; then a sad groan arose from inside the ranch-house. Rand's face was contorted with inexpressible fear and disgust. With a moan closely related to a sob he buried his head in the crook of his arm.

Jeff Rand was a solitary and silent and strong-willed man, who had faced a life of misfortune, hardships and dangers. But now he was beaten. The gang had committed a thorough piece of brutality. There was no hope left for him; and he would have been better dead. Rand's mangled hands resembled jerked hunks of raw meat.

How long he sat there in torment he had never any clear idea. He wanted to wrap the things up again but he had not the strength or courage just then; he wanted to keep them wrapped up for always, because he knew they would never look much different, and that they would surely rouse repugnance and distrust even in a friend. Desire for revenge and inability to take it waged a frustraing war within his breast, almost suffocating him with emotion. Slowly, hesitatingly he again raised his white face and forced himself to look. Those hands were twisted, lacerated, with blue fingernails all displaced, with thumb-joints deformed – they were the cruel talons of a hawk.

'What are you doing, son? You shouldn't have pulled the bandages off. I knowed and said you shouldn't, son.' Ma Keller stood beside him, looking fretful with red-rimmed eyes, and speaking in that soft and husky voice which always thrilled Jeff. 'Try to be patient. They seem worse than they really are, dear me. Them slight fractures can heal up like new, son, if you'll quit trying to bully nature. Sure 'tis no bizness of the Kellers how you came by such brutal mishandling, and you may keep silent if you must. But just remember this, son, that we aim to do duty by our neighbours, as it will never be held agin us nohow.'

'Yes, ma'am. I understand, an' I'm a-telling yez I'm sorry.' mumbled Jeff, glancing quickly up at her then bowing his head. 'Appears like I don't savvy gratitude by one rotten cent.'

'Independence don't get no persons nowhere, son. We all need somebody to lean on sometime. You just keep those hands covered if you're after getting well quick. I'm guessing you have something important to do, and waiting sends you wild. If you're patient, son, and start all over agin to get the grip o' things, you'll soon be trailing away.'

Rand gave her another quick look, wondering how much she meant by 'get the grip o' things'. She made one of those special smiles at him, so that her brown old face became a mass of yellow wrinkles.

'Teresa,' she softly called through the doorway. 'Chase out that jar of salve. We'll truss this man up agin. Everything's all right. He's a-going to quit his boyish pranks in the future.'

She was a fine old lady, and she really understood a fellow; there was none of that sentimental ballyhoo about Ma Keller, but just one big unselfish load of good feelings. So Jeff ruminated watching her return inside, her coarse black skirt rasping against the log wall.

Ma Keller did not know what risk she took harbouring him:

126

and it was this conscience-hounding thought which, the more grand she behaved towards him, kept a-piling more fire into Rand's impatience to recover and ride.

Excitement, increasing daily, began to thrill the remainder of Rand's stay at the ranch. Thanks to Ma and the care of Teresa he was soon forever rid of those maddening bandages; although he knew the sight of his awful talons was a source of grim uneasiness to the good people, they never gave sign of it as he made animal-like fumblings with cutlery at mealtimes, and let fall a couple of coffee mugs. He had to learn again how to use his fingers, to use them naturally, not finding makeshift methods that could grow into awkward habits which would betray he was disabled. He began to plan out a course of exercises to be practised frequently, just like he was a pianoforte player, with the difference that his life would depend on the final test. At times he grew morose, despaired, saw no progress, and was ready to call quits: but it was Teresa's scorn that rallied him to fight on. Whenever he made a little victory, such as opening a can or tying a strap, it was Teresa's praise that spiced his pleasure, deepening his interest, making the situation not miserable but novel. Rand had to learn again how to grip a gun: that was his object in life, and this Teresa failed to consider. He must train to draw swiftly to kill or be killed.

Sometimes behind the woodshed, and sometimes in his room, Rand secretly practised finger exercises for many wearying hours, aiming at a high standard of virtuosity with his instrument, the six-gun. The pain and labour he underwent all alone, with apparently little reward was heartbreaking even for a man naturally swift of action and without his impediments. It seemed ages before he permitted himself to buckle on his gunbelt and seriously try out what he had learned afresh. That day was a kind of crisis for him, a first grade examination.

It was somewhere around noon when Rand stealthily

disappeared behind the stable. He was sweating, trembling, afraid to try it. He had stood an empty can on the broken fence Pa kept threatening to fix, but after glaring somewhat belligerently at it for all of five minutes, his shoulders sagged and he turned away. Then, like a wild-cat released from a snare, he swirled about, dust rose, two guns glittered, spurted, flashed and thundered repeatedly over the Keller's peaceful ranch-house. A piece of torn metal was left plastered to the fence. Rand's eyes glittered wickedly in a face both white and expressionless.

'Good God protect us!'

It was Teresa. She had followed him, seen it happen, yet was not sure, it came so sudden, and now she stood as if paralysed by a strange sickness.

Hearing her exclamation Rand turned sharply, guns smoking. This fresh alarm, peering down those black weapons then at his taut face, caused her to gasp and spill the basket of apples she carried. This was not the man she knew. Gradually Rand appeared to recover from a trance as he watched her, becoming distracted by a quaintly pulsing cord of her neck. The terrible cold gleam faded from his eyes and colour again suffused his face.

'I-I'm sorry, ma'am,' he whispered throatily. 'Thought I spied me a jack-rabbit.'

'A rabbit? On that fence?' she asked, shakily retrieving the fruit.

'Yes, ma'am; on that fence,' Jeff weakly asserted, glancing at the fence to see if it were possible.

Dolefully he returned his guns, grimly aware that never, not since he was a kid in Tucson, had he drawn a gun so slowly.

'Son; is that you, son! Was you a-shooting something, son!'

They could hear Ma calling from the house.

'Best not make her fearful anymore, Mister Rand,' Teresa coldly reproved. 'Luckily Pa's away, gone to Flintstone on the buckboard, else he would be real riled with you. If you must practise guns, we would like warning of it in future, please. I'll try easing Ma with your jack-rabbit talk this time, after hacking away that awkward bit o' fence.'

'Thanks, Teresa. I wouldn't upset the old lady for anything really. I'm more'n grateful to yuh.' He slapped his holsters. 'I'll do my hunting a long stretch from the house after this. Sometimes a fella has to hunt this way to live.'

She had turned to leave but the last remark made her hesitate anxiously.

'Bloodshed's a crazy and dangerous revenge, so I figure, Mister Rand.'

'You've said it, ma'am.'

'The sheriff of Flintstone is paid to run down road-agents that attack poor men like yourself,' she pursued, blushing as she gazed up at him.

'These partic'lar road-agents overpaid me, Teresa,' Rand carefully answered, looking woefully at his hands. 'Being honest, I figure to hand back the change, with interest.'

'Some honesty has a heavy penalty.' Her voice had become tremulous and unconsciously she had drawn near to him; she could almost have touched his poor hands, or even those horrible black guns that frightened her so much.

Rand did not reply. He kept staring down queerly into her eyes, while his heart kept a-throbbing right giddily. She seemed to feel all her secret thoughts being closely studied just then. How long they might have remained there in this fashion was difficult to calculate. But a further call from Ma Keller ended the incident. She shuddered and felt strangely cold as she walked or almost ran away, and Rand's eyes trailed her with the same boring intensity.

CHAPTER FIFTEEN

There was no more gunfire. In secret and silence Rand practised his draw behind the out-buildings. The test had proven
two things: his aim was still excellent, but otherwise he was an
utter failure.

A new routine of life was formed, wherein he only
appeared at mealtimes. After breakfast he tended his horse,
and always carefully avoided Pa lest he was given chores to do.
Then he strolled out on the range for the morning, occasionally taking a pack of grub prepared by Teresa.

If he returned late he sought out Teresa, anxiously asking
if she had seen a strange rider with a fine saddle and a gay
laugh. But whenever Pa tracked him down to mention riding
herd, doing stable work, wood-chopping or well-sinking, then
it was a source of amusement for the women to hear what
complaints Rand could suddenly contract, some of them only
applicable to horses. The very thought of work seemed to
make the fellow ill, more ill than is natural, that is. Rand knew
how work would stiffen fingers already too stiffened. Except
for the horrible look of those hands he was real healthy, with
his face the colour of best quality mahogany, and a springy
liveliness in his stride. Now he never opened a gate or climbed
a fence, he always leapt them. Now he talked less than ever,

but always smiled. It was a peculiar smile, the smile of a man who carries and treasures a secret. The flash of determination in his eyes had changed into a narrow-lidded gleam of hope, as though he at last felt the progress he was making, and had maybe glimpsed his goal.

The gunfighter's recovery was watched with keen interest especially by Teresa, despite her natural repugnance at knowing his private intentions. She could scarcely hide her pleasure to see his health and self-confidence return. Both she and Ma kept defending him mightily against the old man, whose allusions to Rand's bone-laziness grew daily more open and hostile. Ma right plainly packed a load of pity for the gunman, while Pa's suspicions of his guest's bloody profession made him as ill-tempered as a mule in a cactus patch. It was kind of sad to hear the poor old fellow raving when Rand was absent, or just round the corner accidentally overhearing, for in private Rand was slaving like two men, fighting a great battle for self-control and power with a six-gun. Nevertheless, Jeff's hands remained slow and clumsy as everybody could easily witness. They did not respond the same; they stayed deformed, and still looked like the talons of a hawk.

The day arrived when Rand deliberately broke his routine. He did not take much breakfast that morning; he even left Pa to attend his own horse, one thing he had never done before. All the day long he remained at the ranch-house, Pa's rocker kept up an incessant creaking like an old pendulum clock. But Rand was busy, quietly busy, making patterns on paper, then shaping out a piece of high-quality leather, with which he sewed very carefully into his holsters, and stained with berry juice as a kind of disguise.

The sun began to set. The old rancher returned, filled with curiosity, and sank down on the veranda steps to watch Rand finish the work.

131

'Been labouring hard, son?' he asked, a tone of reproach in his voice as he mopped his boiled-looking face. 'Thought I mighta seen you with me at the well today. Water's coming back to the land, but only slow, too derned slow, yet she's sure enough a-coming, son.'

'Sorry, Mister Keller. I thought about your well, then my mind switched on to them bugs and flies – and I felt my malaria rising fast. I had to hold myself back, I might tell yuh.' Jeff looked mournful as he excused himself.

'Shucks, son! Bugs and flies ain't nothing. A fella gets used to the critters. I'm real hardened now, and likes to have their company almost. Hearing them a-buzzing and feeling them crawl keeps yuh cussing, and then you don't feel lonely anymore, and quit worrying about life.' He chuckled and lit his pipe. 'Say, how's that liver complaint, anyhow?'

'Shaping,' admitted Jeff. 'Shaping nicely, thanks.'

'Huh! Never had a one in all my life,' the old fellow proudly declared, staring with odd determination at the horizon. 'Hard work warded 'em off I reckon. All I ever suffer from is poverty, all along o' my staying on to fight that blamed desert. Everybody quit 'cept me and old man James with fifty-odd cows. He died. I even beat him.' He chuckled again, more proudly. 'Yep; but just when I'm fixing to build up the old place now the dust's drifting off, I have to sell out.' His voice began to shake, implying hidden anger and sorrow. 'When those blood-sucking hoodlums cleaned out Flintstone bank, son, they flattened out old man Keller. I'm broke.'

Rand was unprepared to hear this tragedy: for once his face betrayed him. He flushed in what might have been guilty confusion, and the gunbelt he worked on slipped from his knee.

'A raw deal that there, Pa,' he managed to mutter. 'When do you break up the old homestead?'

132

'In the fall,' the old-timer replied, hiding his grief by lifting and studying Rand's gunbelt. ' 'Cept for that crime I could have hired cowpokes next year, real hard workers I mean.' He stressed the last words for Jeff's benefit. 'You see, when folk ran before the desert, they took to digging gold. I scorned them for it; they were ranchers not miners. They were doing a wrong thing. Ranching is your honest-to-goodness living, I said. Stay and fight. Keep your homes. Damn the gold!' He puffed furiously at his pipe, and then dejectedly went on, 'But now they're sitting pretty, son, and I'm the poor fool because I did right. Lucky devils, all of 'em. Say, was you ever at the diggings? I hate them.'

'Yeah, Pa. I'm a gold digger.' confessed Jeff.

'There! See what I mean? Everybody's the same. And I bet you and your kin are right down rich,' argued the rancher.

'No, just murdered,' Rand purred the evil word.

The old man snatched his pipe from his mouth and looked shocked. He found difficulty in digesting a sudden remorse.

'Well, well, well! Have you nobody then, son; no pardner nor nothing?'

'Murdered!' Rand sounded more forbidding.

Pa Keller looked even more distressed. He wanted to sympathise, but gentle emotion like that never came easy to him. At this moment he could only hate himself for a talkative old croak, a buffer, or any other name fitting a tomfool crackpot. Rand's manner, as he gave him a side-long look, was sending a queer thrill through his aged bones, same feeling he got last year when he found the well dried up and a snake at the bottom.

Giving a nervous cough Pa stretched out a horny hand and stroked the new leather work on Rand's belt.

'Knowed a gunslinger once as used this same slick leather on his holsters,' he drawled amiably. 'His name was Ives, worst cut-throat of the infamous Plummer Gang. Gunmen aren't nowheres as fast as in the old days. Men are getting lazier and slower of action, because of lucky strikes, I reckon. George Ives was hanged at Nevada City.'

Rand took back the gunbelt and buckled it on.

'Seen any strangers on the range today, Pa,' he mildly asked.

'Not yet,' answered Keller, forcibly restraining his curiosity. 'Few fellows ever ride through here now. But mebbe yonder's the man you want.'

Pointing to a single rider cantering through a distant patch of sage-brush, the rancher arose and wearily descended the steps. He failed to notice Rand's shocked face, and did not hear him ease himself out of the rocker and glide into the house.

A moment later Rand was watching proceedings through a ventilator in the small store room.

'Hi, Sheriff! Wondered when you'd honour us agin,' he heard Pa call out. 'Let's huck down here where it's cooler.'

Rand heard Pa's step on the veranda, followed by the heavier football of a short and broad middle-aged man. The sheriff's hands were interestingly white. Unthinkingly Rand slid his own hands in his pockets and listened closely.

'Glad to see you, Pa,' boomed the famous sheriff of Flintstone as he began to swing in the rocker with a certain familarity. 'Sunk another well, I see.'

'Yes, and the water's seeping in, slow but sure, Bill. Even the old lake will come back, that's a prophecy. Things will be just like when you was foreman.'

'Sure it will, Pa. 'Pend on that. How's the old lady and the gal?' inquired the sheriff, lowering his voice. 'Have you told 'em?'

'They're bearing up well.' Pa sounded uneasy. 'I

134

mentioned being broke, off-handedly. I didn't say how broke, not a word about the hold-up, or selling out.'

In the store-house Rand, fearful of Ma or Teresa entering to serve something to the visitor, dared hardly move among the hanging pieces of crockery. He could have reached out and touched the sheriff's smartly-plastered hair.

'Hang fire with your sad news,' continued the sheriff. 'Mebbe you won't have to sell. Mebbe I'll lay-low that bank-busting gang afore long. Wait and see.'

'Got a rope stretched for 'em, have you, Bill?' Pa began prying. 'What's your scheme?'

'Don't sell out, that's all,' the sheriff firmly told him again. 'Well now, have you seen any strangers around?'

'Strangers, strangers, strangers! Everybody asking for strangers. Who do you fellows expect here, the president or something?' Pa's pipe was sending up furious smoke-signals once more. 'Like I told Jeff only a moment gone, nobody comes here now.'

That was enough; that did it. Rand could hide no longer. He must get out of here and ride. A few moments more and that sheriff would know everything and come a-searching. The time to ride had arrived before he was ready, before his hands were fully prepared: and he hadn't even tried out these new-style holsters.

He turned to leave; a couple of hanging milk-jugs jangled together; Teresa opened the door, and found herself in Jeff's arms.

'Bring my hoss round the rear,' he muttered.

'But – but why?' she asked, trembling against him as he thrust her out.

'My hoss!' he commanded.

'Do as he says, Teresa,' Ma Keller softly interrupted from the outer doorway; she was wearing a shawl for the evening was chilly and there was a flash of excitement in her eyes. 'Come here, son,' she added, giving him a pathetic look while Teresa departed. 'Be careful. You just ain't ready for it.'

'I know, Ma, I know!' he spoke impatiently; then he looked at her sharply, surprised at her penetration. How much did she guess?

She stood regarding him steadily and gravely, the side of her wrinkled mouth twitching nervously. Rand felt his exterior hardness crumbling away as she seemed to go mining after his true self. He muttered irritably to himself, wrung his terrible hands together and looked away. He was afraid he might show how scared he really was; he was afraid he might suddenly embrace the grand old lady.

With a choking sense of gratitude, Rand obviously yearned to say many kind things to her, and to give parting respects to Pa, yet he could say nothing. He retreated backward to the rear door, seeming kind of entranced by the gentle encouraging smile on the old woman's face. Teresa had by now returned, hot and breathless. She stood in the shadow beside that door, and there were tears in her wide, staring eyes. He glanced quickly at her. Thereat she thrust a parcel of food into his hands, upon which hands she fixed her attention with such mounting tender emotion as would have alarmed any man.

'Whereabouts is Sweetwater?' he abruptly asked with a queer huskiness.

If Rand had dived for his guns and explosively shattered the strained peace of the moment, the two women could barely have looked more horrified. The old woman's smile vanished; tightly she clutched her shawl around her narrow shoulders as if she felt the breath of Winter. Teresa uttered a cry of dismay.

'What's the matter? Where's Sweetwater? Hurry! Please

136

quit the foolin', Ma!' Rand whispered in growing desperation: the creaking of the rocking chair had ceased out on the veranda.

'Sweetwater! It's a hell-pot! Don't go, son!' the old woman croaked oddly; and, continuing to deplore the place as a den of iniquity, she extended a trembling hand westwards.

'Goodbye, Ma,' whispered Rand, sharply swinging around. 'Goodbye!'

'Rand!' Teresa screamed his name as she released feelings long held secretly in check. 'Come back, Rand!'

A lone rider was streaking across the parched range-land, with his own name echoing sadly in his ears. The price for a recent slice of happiness was giving a mighty power of pain, and the pain was reforming an old resolution. No, Rand would always run wild, always ride alone. He headed for the desert.

CHAPTER SIXTEEN

A desolate region marked the outer edges of Keller's one-time booming cattle country, a land of dust, prickly-pears and antique oxen skulls. Through this sad scenery rode Jeff Rand, heading directly west into the sea-like setting of the desert sun. His mission was death.

Being on horse-back again imparted a relieving sense of security; he felt at home where he belonged, instead of getting all awkward and shy of manners among homesteaders and decent peace-abiding folk like the Kellers. For a man like himself the ground was dangerous. Thus the first dozen or so miles of galloping gave a right smart uplift to Rand's spirits; but as he progressed further, as the sun submerged itself and the stars inherited the heavens, shining chilly over the running sand, he began to consider more profoundly the object of his ride. Thereat he was possessed by an awful sinking sensation in the body. He knew then that he was going to die.

Beyond a certain expanse of cacti and Spanish-nettles he dismounted for a while. According to his calculating it was close on two a.m. Sweetwater should be located, if Ma Keller had pointed in the right direction, somewhere around dayrise. There was no hurry, however; the end would come soon enough. No doubt Ives, the old gunman Pa had mentioned, felt just this same way afore being hanged. Debating in this way, Rand kept himself company; and his argufying ended by praising Teresa's goodness. She had slung fat water-skins across his saddle, which he now found excellently cooling. He also chuckled at the piece of knitting she had confusedly bundled among the provisions. He smelt it, stretched it with animal-like curiosity, then hucked down to brood and drink and chew dried apples.

Of a sudden he stiffened alertly: a horse's hoof had struck flint, way out there in the blackness.

'Sheriff's men,' he muttered, first spitting out a mouthful of fruit as he stretched himself upon his stomach.

For a long while he spied nothing, until he happened to peer eastward. Then he perceived about thirty riding shapes moving against the starlit sky. They were drowsily steering a course for Vulch City.

'Miners,' Rand breathed. 'Miners what are rarin' to lynch a fella; you bet. They are boiling mad for Bruce Gang blood, and aching to get back to their diggings. Disturbing man, that sheriff. He don't quit easy. He must guess the gang ain't yet crossed the border.'

Presently Rand was back in the saddle again, and riding due west. A couple of hours lapsed by before he made out a cloud-like outline of mountains over to the left.

'Grapevine Gulch, twenty miles south, mebbe more,' he idly murmured, reaching forward to stuff dried apples into the horse's mouth, then wiping his slobbery hand on its mane. 'Touch of frost in the air. The falls a-coming. Poor Pa Keller! Selling out the old place. Darned shameful thing. There's Grapevine now! That tall monument of stone is like a tombstone for Smily. He was a fine boy. He hadn't a chance. Symes just. . . .'

But recollection of that gunfight, of the terrible death-dealing swiftness of Symes, caused Rand's gorge to rise in fresh dread.

'With yuh soon, Smily,' he snarled, trying to be tough with himself. 'Yeah; you too Jim Miller. And I'm a-bringing company for hell.'

He gave the animal a nervous slap; it grunted and cantered more resolutely over the rolls of sand.

Riding, riding, riding across ever grimmer looking territory; sometimes searching all directions, most times nodding, jerking up in alarm, taking another swig of water, often feeling gun-butts, then peering woefully at distorted hands – under such occupation as this did Rand while away the time. In half-dreams he pictured the people he had met since Jim Miller died; and finally he ruminated on his last moments with the Bruce Gang. Again he asked himself the old problem: whose brain really operated the outfit? Again the same solution was reached: the man who held Miller's watch was boss – the same man Sturdy whose gun he still felt in his back just before that last fight in the storm. Nevertheless Sturdy's move had saved him from being cruelly slain. But the move had been made for a greedy purpose; no doubt Sturdy was hoping Rand would return to cut down his enemies, thus saving a wasteful share-out of dollars. Reaching this dreamy conclusion, Rand once more jerked up in alarm, and looked behind. A tingling thrill passed through his body. Already he was being pursued by the light of dawn.

Newly alert and anxious his searching eyes roved ahead. Somewhere in the darkness yonder this foul desert must be merging into grassland. He broke into a steady gallop, his intention being to get into town before the citizens began to stir.

About thirty minutes later Rand drew rein, dismayed to

see, by the spreading paleness, a seemingly endless panorama of desolation. Mound followed mound on every side. Furthermore he kept glimpsing dark forms soaring overhead, circling lower and lower: he was being haunted by death-forseeing vultures. The atmosphere just hereabout was something more than melancholy – it was downright sinister. As he again scanned the distance his blood ran cold: his horse began to tremble under him; an uncanny moaning and sighing was creeping out of the sand.

Never in his life had Rand been afraid of loneliness. Yet here at this hour both he and that wise old horse were sure uneasy about the unknown. The whole district was empty in the purple shade; the moaning died away; all was as silent as the stars again, with a deadness seeming just as ancient. Rand could now feel his heart drumming under stress of danger.

First it was a little movement nearby that attracted his notice: a red leaf on a thorn branch was twisting round and round in the motionless air, as if by a secret mechanism. Gradually the deceptive light expanded, hounding away the shadows, until Rand next spied little holes appearing in the sand, like the holes in a frying flapjack. Then the sighing breathed forth again, turned into a snake-like hiss – the holes multiplied, spread rapidly around him – the desert was draining off, vanishing under his horse. Suddenly, jolting his heart into his throat, there came an ominous crackling and snapping.

Digging spurs into his mount, he leapt free. Next instant the place collapsed. Haggard and white of face, Rand drew up and gazed back. A black chasm yawned up at him. He could see rotten planks, and deep below were rows of bottles, winking like eyes, while around them lay heaps of bones. Slowly and terribly realisation came like the dawning around him – he had been standing on a cabin roof; and, as he watched the sand filtering from the remainder of it, he could read the following gaudy lettering:

SWEETWATER SALOON

It took a considerable while before Jeff Rand overcame the shakes that had attacked him, quietened his horse, and got down to thinking straight and to surveying his surroundings with more particularity. He was standing amidst a half-buried town, dead in the centre of the Bruce Gang's hideout.

Two lines of mounds, similar to the one he had been standing upon, extended right and left before him: this apparently had been the main street. As his gaze travelled down it he could make out sections of stove-pipe protruding from the sand, further on roof-tops showed like a fleet of half-sunken river-boats. At the extreme end of the town the shacks stood comparatively free, their lifeless windows and doors giving them a ghoulish appearance. Old Ma Keller had been dead right when she said:

'Sweetwater is a hell-pot. Sweetwater packed more sin than a full-blowed city, so she got smote and clean Godforsaken.'

Now, as Jeff Rand viewed that scene with an even deeper feeling of foreboding with Ma's words a-ringing in his ears, the yellow sunlight came and tinged everything like a sickly disease, while spooky shadows got to haunting behind those distant buildings, and while the stillness and quietude continued as if in eternal mourning for the dead. He decided to do something; if he just sat there looking he would get too scared to do anything except run away.

'Best take a quick squint round,' he whispered softly to himself. 'Won't go far, though, too derned gruesome. Wonder why they calls it Sweetwater. Don't seem to be no water no place, sweet nor sour; and no life neither; no Bruce Gang just no nothing.'

Whilst he hesitated a moment longer to bite into a chaw of tobacco, a thin taper of blue smoke started to breathe straight upward from one of the furthermost buildings.

'Whoa, Jeff!' He paused with the tobacco clenched in his teeth. 'They're still here. That's a funny thing.'

He sounded calm and self-possessed, when actually the old quaking sensation was at it again, but now operating like the gripes.

'Why ain't they shooting at me? Lookouts must have spied me by this time. Mebbe Bruce and his boys are waiting till I'm well in and sealed afore blasting.'

He checked over his guns, transferred a certain mining certificate from a pocket into a saddle-bag, then plodded with lazy slowness down the main street of Sweetwater.

'Townfolk sure left in a hurry,' he observed, his quick eyes flashing into passing doorways, noting broken furniture, and even searching out sand-filled mugs and pans, and tables spread for some long forgotten meal. 'Say, just look there! Now that's real weird.' Mournfully he beheld the rising ground to the left of town, where lay a half-submerged wagon train complete with sun-bleached skeletons of oxen. 'You know what? A thing like that could scare a normal fella. I'm real scared. Yeah, but I wonder what lies behind that great rift o' dust. An army could huck down there and bushwhack another army, so to speak.' He plodded past the rift which extended from the stables to the stage-office. 'All clear!' he breathed. 'Whole cabins are showing up now. How-dee, how-dee! The smoke's stopped. Which building had it been belching from, anyhow? And where. . . . What the blazes!'

There came a stunning crash. A hot blast of air rushed past him. Rand's guns were half-drawn; his body was twisted in the saddle; furiously he sat regarding a certain window shutter, swinging loosely in the sudden charge of wind.

143

'Nasty shock, that there!' he grunted, moving on with eyes still wide. 'Sun's fading afore it's even ripe. Wind's coming in earnest; dust clouds in the south; looks bad, but it won't be much. Reckon I'll make for yonder Hurdy Gurdy House.'

More hot rushes of air set that shutter slamming behind him with dismal regularity. Little eddies of sand and rubbish scuttered in and out of gloomy doorways. Further on a liquor dealer's cabin set up a swaying and squeaking like a tombful of devils in a brawl. Right opposite stood the Belmont Hotel, lopsided and roofless. Next door, looking more substantial and habitable, was the Hurdy Gurdy House, a haunt of wildly gay memories, and it happened to be the chosen hideout of the Bruce Gang.

A hideout in Sweetwater had been a very shrewd choice; no posse would give the place a second thought: Sweetwater was dead, empty, buried, offering no refuge; and surely no living man would have nerve enough to lay low in a den of evil spirits. Since Sweetwater was Godforsaken the devil had taken over, lock, stock and barrel, not to mention normal spooks.

'We ain't seen nothing, dead nor alive in weeks, 'cepting the local population of lizards and bugs, and a wandering phantom or two.' So complained many of the gang with tempers frayed. 'We've gotten ourselves a fat load o' dollar bills, yet we suffer real awful poverty and won't get a pauper's burial at this rate, what with hungry guts hanging out, dried up livers and all, not to mention lumbago and attacks of scratchy-back. By hell!'

'Wish you boys would quit foolin' around.' Big Bruce was savagely snarling, as he sat jerking beans out of a can at the bar. 'Give me some coffee, Gowl. This filth is lousy; feels like I'm being hanged.'

'Coffee, coffee, coffee! Don't he do nothin' but drink that

bilge?' grumbled Clay, who had apparently acquired a delicate taste during his late saloon-sweeping days.

'Never mind that. You hand back my soap, Clay, and watch your own affairs!' roared Mex, his brawny body stripped to the waist and flecked with lather from the razor he brandished at Clay's face. 'Give back. I say give or I cut ears off Meester Clay!'

With a frightened curse and a stagger, Clay retreated as the frothy razor flicked dangerously close to his eyes.

'Slice him up, Mex! Cut him to stew-meat!' Symes urged in a rapture from his bunk, which was the top of an old square piano. 'Slit his beeg fat tongue, Mexy boy. Then have a nice clean wash for old time's sake.'

'Quit foolin', all of yuh!' Bruce bawled more loudly. 'Gowl has plenty of soap to go round, he even thickens the coffee with the stuff, fear it goes to waste. Just go easy on the water, Mex, that's all. Why shave, anyhow? Nobody else does.'

' 'Cept me,' yawned Symes, stretching out again, a little disappointed in Mex. 'I even get me a wash.' This was true; somehow Symes had mysteriously preserved a well groomed look. 'There's only one other thing required, Bruce, and that's for Mister Sturdy to ride back safe, saying the search is off.'

'Don't worry, Symes. Sturdy is clever. I'm glad he drew the ace when we cut cards for it.' Bruce sipped thoughtfully at his coffee and soap. 'It's like being in lousy Noah's lousy Ark, being penned up in here, and sending a fella out to check land this fashion. Never mind, soon as we get word the sheriff's gathered himself enough saddle-corns, soon as he goes back to his red-hot town, then we'll ride slick across the border. Then comes the share-outs and a rip-snorting life.'

'You bet. We've earned it,' agreed Winters, eager to please Bruce after the whipping he had received at the gulch.

'Look here, boss,' said Gowl, leaning persuasively over the bar. 'Just because I wasn't on the raid doesn't mean I get a thin cut, I hope. My job's important. Without grub you'd all die, then where would you be? Wherefore I figures I've kind of saved your lives, getting all these supplies out here. Wherefore with Larry swallowed up in the storm, and numbers now being what they are, my slice should be – erm – thick.'

Bruce grinned largely into his face, raised a can of boiling coffee, and slowly poured the liquid over Mister Gowl's head.

'You poison me, same as this bilge,' he whispered confidentially, shaking out the last dregs, and thoroughly enjoying everybody's laughter as the cook, howling pitifully, leapt back in agony.

'Big and beautiful wads o' bills, fellas,' drawled Symes, heartlessly ignoring the incident, and now standing on the piano to turn out the kerosene lamp. 'Then comes the fine food, the peach brandy – and the gals.'

'Did anyone hear them noises agin, last night?' asked Tom, nervously shuffling a pack of cards.

'Don't interrupt me, Tom; it's naughty,' Symes coldly reproached him, his black eyes glaring wide. 'Lay off the whiskey, Tom, then the spooks will hightail it.'

' 'Tain't just whiskey, neither,' argued Gowl, sounding spiteful and breathless, with an old shirt round his half-boiled head. 'I was reared here in Sweetwater; there now. This town's bad medicine today, and yesterday it was worse than Deadwood is today, and that's talking some, I can tell you. There used to be shootings and stabbings no end, drink came cheap, and every citizen from kids upward became a roistering drunk at sundown. I ain't lying, boys. Sin up and slaughtered most townfolk, and what sin didn't get the desert did. Why, there's hundreds o' skeletons in this here sand, under your boots.'

'What a low-down dry place to end up!' Symes mildly exclaimed, sending a stream of tobacco juice across the mortuary floor.

A great roar of laughter greeted the remark.

'Ah, but I'm serious,' Gowl gravely argued.

'You're sand-crazy,' snorted Bruce. 'Here, have some more coffee.' He reached for a steaming can.

'You leave me alone,' warned the cook, glancing towards a hatchet.

'Say, don't you get worked up?' Bruce muttered. 'Take care, Mister, because my fists have grown hungry since pounding that sham gunman's bones.'

'Jeengo, but Rand was sure soft and messy under the fist!' scorned Mex, dabbing a greasy rag at his shaven chin. 'I can feel him now.'

'His gun-dragging days are over,' the boss firmly declared, relishing his memories. 'I crunched his finger-bones dead.'

'Shut up!' Symes' face wore a menacing look as he sprang upright on the piano. 'Quit that talk, Brucy boy! It makes my hands itch!'

A tensed silence followed, with Bruce flushed, looking surprised, as if he had foolishly sat on something hot and didn't want it to get around. He wanted to be angry, only fear lowered his temperature.

During the silence they heard a far-away banging of a shutter. Thereat Bruce released his passion, by shying a can of beans at Clay.

'Next time I order you to fix something, do it!' he roared. 'Listen to that infernal shutter.'

'Gives me the creeps, so it do,' whispered Tom.

'Me too. Winds hereabouts are queersome things,' agreed Mex.

147

'Hush! Listen! Shut your jaws!' snapped Symes, squirting tobacco juice at the bean can meant for Clay's head, then cupping a hand to his ear.

'What's the matter? Hear something, do yuh?' whispered Bruce.

'Loads o' skeletons, boys, right under your feet,' Gowl spitefully repeated in a low voice.

Nobody paid any attention to him; all listened to the banging and squeaking. It seemed to be drawing nearer and nearer. Presently the commotion developed with a wicked frenzy. A tremendous hissing broke out close by. Next instant a terrible power started to shake the old mouldering building.

'Just the fool wind,' Bruce laughed forcibly.

Now the sand came, fizzing like fine grain through every slit betwixt the wall-boards. The sun went out. A peculiar humming came from the doorway; the doorway became choked by a whirling cloud of sand – and the cloud grew denser.

'Look! Good God! Look there!'

Everybody jolted where he sat or sprawled; everybody stared as Big Bruce, screaming to be heard above the racking din, pointed with outstretched arm.

'What in hell is it?' someone yelled, terror in his voice.

The sand cloud was retreating; the sounds were subsiding. But now a tall and haggard figure, appearing then fading alternately, mutely watched them from the doorway of the Hurdy Gurdy House.

CHAPTER SEVENTEEN

Bloodshed, huntger, thirst, a long trail of sufferings, not to mention the present sojourn in Sweetwater, had been endured for the obtaining of 'easy money'. But exactly how worn down was the Bruce Gang's nerve at the present stage of its existence, only became apparent now on beholding that grim apparition in the doorway. Such was the shock produced, that Jeff Rand might have just risen from the grave.

'Who killed Miller?' Rand's voice revealed his identity, lashing them back to realities.

'Hi-there, Jeff!' Symes recovered first, and, still squatting on the piano, he waved a hand in friendly style. 'Knowed somehow you'd pay a call.'

'Which of you lousy snakes killed my pardner and stole my gold?' Rand repeated in the same booming tones; and taking one forward step he more fully revealed himself.

Nobody answered. Everybody watched. They knew death was waiting hungrily in that place. Bruce had now balled his huge fists and his white face leered at the accusing visitor. Mex slyly rested a hand in readiness on his knife. Clay, Winters, Tom and Gowl kept tensed, close to their guns. Symes alone looked at ease, watching the scene with a ridiculously stupid face, feigning innocence.

149

'Come back for your share-out, have you, Sham?' Bruce spoke with utmost scorn, striving to control his rage.

'Who killed Miller?'

Once more the question snarled across the room. Yet Rand was trembling inwardly. There seemed to be so many of them, not to mention that gun-wizard Symes. Nor had Jeff entered with drawn guns; in fact his shock on finding them in this building had equalled if not exceeded that of the whole outfit. But guns, drawn or holstered, did not matter much just then; he could not kill them all. Bruce and Symes would satisfy him. He might not even get any of them: Symes created that secret terror. Yet Rand had resigned himself to death from the beginning, even before he left the ranch-house. Whereas the idea was fresh and shocking to these fellows, who looked forward to a luxurious future. What a fine old man was Keller! How grand was the old lady! Queer he should think of them at this terrible moment. Maybe they were thinking of him, Teresa too. Maybe this moment was part of a preformed plan of his life, all starting off when he was a kid, revenging his poor kinfolk. What a heartbreak for a fellow, after so many years gunfighting and careful watching, to end up right here with this pack of wretched hoodlums. Rand prepared himself to die.

'Bruce!' The name came like a bark. 'Busting that bank, using my gold, opened the gates o' hell. But by mauling me, busting my hands, you have drawn out the flames. Make your play, Mister, and burn!'

'You streak of filth! I shoulda broken your neck as well!' Bruce almost shrieked in his wrath; his bared chest was bulging and heaving in passion. He first poured forth all the profane language he could before emotion choked him. 'A gun – gimme a gun, somebody!' he then hissed viciously. 'Look! See his hands! Just hunks of rotten meat. Ha-ha-haa!

150

His stinkin' paws couldn't hold sticks, let alone his guns. I'll finish him myself. Blast yuh, Clay! Hurry! Gimme a gun!'

A six-shooter was spun across. Bruce caught it adeptly, laughing in fiendish joy. Then it happened. Rand vanished. He stepped back into the curtain of sand, and Bruce fired instantly. Two flaming streams of lead ripped back from the doorway.

Rand suddenly materialised again, a changed man, a merciless wild beast. His face was taut, his eyes were staring and blazing, and his claw-like hands clenched two guns, belching death.

'I'm with yuh, Jeff!' A voice raised itself impressively in the thunderous uproar, followed by the crashing down of a piano. 'Come on, Jeff! We'll clean up these filthy savages together!'

Sand flew, gunsmoke whirled, someone was laughing hideously, someone else kept shrieking in agony. About a dozen guns open-fired, resounding their terrifying message in the walls. The uproar, grinding in one's ears, was simply stupefying. Every man's heart contracted, quaked in fear for his flesh, as he took part in the battle.

Rand had lunged in fearlessly, sending bullets slicing into Bruce's barrel of a chest. Bruce staggered, hideous in shock, hideous in the dying sensation that possessed him. He was sinking down, pressing a thumb into an oozing hole.

'Symes!' he groaned, trying to re-aim his gun. 'I kill you! You cheat – fraud – damn thief – hell!'

His massive body crashed to the floor, shaking the house.

In the same instant a knife was shattered in mid-air. Rand's guns were on Mex; and Mex, now weaponless, felt something hot tearing softly through his neck.

The bullet-pierced mirrors of the Hurdy Gurdy House multiplied the enemy. There was no place to hide except behind the fallen piano – and Clay was there; and except

151

behind the bar – and Gowl lurked there. Rand ceased firing. He staggered, looked stupefied, and stood swaying groggily, ready to pitch down headlong. Vaguely he was aware of someone beside him; someone who laughed crazily; someone who stood boldly erect, feet astride and unmindful of shots ripping through his fine clothing. It was Symes. What was he doing? He was holding his guns carelessly, yet firing with enjoyable deliberation, steadily killing his own friends. Now the bodies thudded down, visibly bleeding, writhing and taking more lead. Now the enemy shrieked in mingled surprise and agony. Yes, it was Symes before them, Symes on Rand's side, and Rand was scarcely less shocked than the Bruce Gang meeting death. A great hush embraced the Hurdy Gurdy House. What? Was it all over already? Rand, who had not even emptied his guns, was answered by that all-smothering and unearthly silence. It was the end.

A last piece of glass tinkled from the mirror behind the bar. An eddy of sand hissed round a paper bag, and a flexible whisp of powder fume trailed through a slit in the wall-boards. It was cold in here now. Outside the storm still raged pretty bad, but it seemed strangely remote, buried deep by this interior silence.

Something started to moan real gruesomely behind the bar. A blood-smeared figure slowly rose up, wheezing, and gaping in terror at the two gunfighters who stood out there, grimly reviewing their terrible work.

'Fetch a – fetch a doctor!' Gowl groaned in a joggling voice, appealing to them. 'Please – hurry – bring a sawbones, someone!'

A low chuckle answered him.

'No, no, Mister! Don't kill me! You get the money, every cent. I get a doctor; just fetch a doctor.'

'Sure, neighbour. Doctor a-coming up!'

Lazy footsteps thudded towards the bar.

'No, no, no!' Gowl screamed.

The footsteps arrived, and stopped.

'Quit that, Symes!' Rand called out faintly, shielding his glazed eyes, and shaking his fuddled head.

'No, mister, no! Dear God, no, Mister Symes!'

As Gowl begged in naked terror, looking stark and staring, he felt his hair grasped. His head was jerked down upon the counter, and the counter smelt rotten and mouldy, spiced like coffin-wood. Releasing another chuckle, Symes shot Gowl through the skull.

'No gang, no risks, no shares!' he lilted, spinning and holstering his weapon. 'Pull yourself together, Jeff. We two make a rare army. There's a fortune in yon piano-forty, so let's load and ride. I've got the guns, you've got the guts, so we both get the money.'

Gleeful and business-like, Symes stepped over Big Bruce's body and, lifting the piano lid, he began to haul out saddle-bags, heavy with dollars.

'Funny thing, you showing up right on time, Jeff, same as if prefixed atween us. Mind you, I had it all figured out this way back at Grapevine. Though I didn't care to spring the plan and give you the layout till we bust the bank and sat pretty here. Then unluckily you fell foul of snake's flesh there. But never mind, Jeff. We don't care one cuss now. Jest look at this! The jackpot!'

Still dazed, the gun-battle continuing to thunder in his head, Rand watched and listened, hardly believing in the altered situation, barely able to credit that he had escaped through it unscathed. Sure enough he felt baffled and drunk, a natural thing after an illness. But – but what about Symes? Just listen to him yapping like a fool kid playing hookey, catching fish. What was he saying, anyhow? Why was he flinging those bags out on the veranda?

Realization rushed in of a sudden, clearing the mental cloud like sunshine, levelling his course, and exposing danger. His position was no better than if these dead men had risen and confronted him with reloaded guns. Symes still lived.

'Get some water-bags ready, Jeff,' called out Symes, 'and bundle together a few supplies. I'm off to get horses; they're penned up in the Belmont.'

He headed for the door as he gave the orders.

'Hang on a moment, mister!' yelled Rand.

He was too late, however; Symes had already hurried into the street and the deafening wind. When Rand reached the veranda, almost stumbling over the heap of saddle-bags thereon, and nearly blinded by flying grit, Symes was halfway to the roofless Belmont Hotel, the gang's stable.

'Sy-y-ymes!' he called, cupping his hands to his mouth. 'Come back, you big-headed fool! Stop!'

The freak sand-storm was easing off, yet already the flying dust had piled like snow against the heap of bulging saddle-bags, and was blowing irritatingly up Rand's rawhide pants. The main street, previously hoof-marked, was again like an untouched Christmas scene, except where Symes left his criminal footsteps as he hastened over to the hotel.

'Sy-y-ymes!'

Rand shouted once more, and on this occasion the wind caught up and freighted his call, rising and falling. The distantly swaggering gunman halted. Puzzled and ever cautious he stood in crooked thought for a second or two, previous to turning slowly around. Rand then came down the broken steps and struck out towards him, yelling loudly as he went.

'The money's all yours, Sy-y-ymes! Every rotten dime is

154

yours. I ain't after nothing, 'cept my own gold. You are riding out alone.'

Symes heard and bowed his head. He traced a toe in the sand and reflected a while.

'Jeff, I admires kind natures like yorn.' He suddenly looked up and yelled back. 'But you see, sonny, I knows the money's all mine. Your hand-out is the gold. After services I make the pay-off. You ride with me.'

Rand, plainly astonished at this reply, halted about twenty-five paces from him.

'You know what, Symes? A fellow might distrust them services you mention, and the pay-off. A fellow might figure you aimed to leave him just this side of the border, with empty saddle-bags, and saddle. With nothing but a bullet in the back!'

'Lordy, lordy me!' Symes seemed to appreciate Rand's vivid imagination. 'What a wicked bad mind you have, Jeff!'

'Sorry,' Jeff apologised, not smiling, but pale and agitated. 'You see, Symes, I am also an evil-minded thinker. You'd be safer without a cuss like me. Just hand over my gold and I'll ride.'

'Fiddlesticks, Jeff! Don't be cruel mean with yourself,' Symes appealed to him. 'You're my only witness, old pardner; so don't get awkward and go and commit suicide on me.' He paused, kicked sand over the design he had traced with his toe, then proceeded in altered accent. 'We ride out together.'

'Mister Symes,' said Rand.

'Yes, Jeff?' asked Symes.

'I don't like you. I ain't a-coming, because you make me sick.'

At that remark Symes' body tensed, and he instinctively sought a firmer footing in the sand. Their argument had reached a deadlock. A desperate and frightening war of looks was waged, more intense than ever previous.

Rand stood bent-shouldered, and as perfectly still as he could in the streaming wind. His face had turned expression-less, no longer grimacing at the stinging grit; and his awful hands, hooked like claws in his waistcoat pockets, instinctively flexed themselves, like two separate evil creatures.

'Who killed Miller?'

The question was launched shakily yet loudly.

Symes received the question and instantly he crouched lower.

'Who – killed – Miller?'

More loudly and less shakily the words ran on the wind. Symes snarled inwardly, and he seemed to be bristling like a wild-cat in deadly readiness.

'WHO – KILLED – MILLER?'

With unbelievable volume and passion the words roared from Jeff Rand's throat.

A brief pause ensued. Then came the answer.

'There's your man,' shouted a familiar voice, stern with authority. 'You are facing him.'

Both men glanced sharply aside, and were momentarily astounded to see Mister Sturdy standing there on the side-walk. Beside Sturdy, holding two horses by the bridles, and beholding the scene with deepest gravity, was the sheriff of Flintstone.

'Bruce robbed the old prospector, Mister Rand, and Symes shot him down in cold blood.' Sturdy tried to keep the hatred out of his voice. 'I bear witness to the malicious killing of James Miller.'

Livid with fury, Symes posted Sturdy a venomous look, a look that gleamed with a desire to kill him. He quickly returned his attention to Rand, keen to see how he received the information. Rand's face was blank, yet his hands had

156

become stiffly extended.

'Throw down your guns, Mister Symes,' commanded the sheriff. 'I carry a warrant for your arrest, brought by a US marshal.'

The sheriff had dived a hand into his pocket for the document, but some silently-thrilling communication between both these men out there, warned him not to withdraw that hand. He could do nothing, except anxiously devour the terrible play being enacted before him.

Rand did not think to question the mysterious change in Sturdy, now on the side of the law; he did not need to question Sturdy, he wanted no more evidence than that which Symes had already given by silence. Despite his exterior coldness as he now awaited the moment of action, Rand was sickened with fear. His eyes kept glazing over so that Symes faded before him. Moreover he felt a queer paralysis extending down his arms. He couldn't help picturing how Smily had died before the matchless Symes. How could he beat such swiftness? How could he even move? But wait! Had he remembered to reload after the battle? He did not recollect. Sweat, itching trickles of salty sweat ran down his face. Symes was ready – any moment now – then death.

'He won't make it! Jeff can't beat him! Look at his hands!' Mister Sturdy could not contain his excitement as he whispered to the sheriff, gripping his arm.

'Poor man! Hands like a damned hawk!' the horrified sheriff muttered fiercely. 'Yeah; a gun-hawk!'

For perhaps the first time in his bloody career, Symes was assailed by a passing doubt as he watched Rand's pose. Yonder fellow certainly had a load of real courage; but he was a fool. He had watched Rand in action against Crocker, and found him barely average. But now, with fingers like gnarled roots, what chance had he? Symes was nonetheless strangely fascinated by those hands; from their distorted appearance he conceived a sickly haunting dread. He looked this fear full in the face, and scorned it. He was too experienced to be caught that way. It died a natural death. Symes started to laugh balefully to himself. Then drew.

His guns leapt up, sprang to him, and roared in rapid succession.

Rand's hands had not moved. They still seemed to be hooked in his waistcoat; and yet, he held his guns. Miraculous guns; guns that darted to him like living things; and guns whose flaming shots pounded like bolts from hell. Bullets twittered by his legs as, emptying every chamber, his victim fell firing to earth. Symes' face showed disbelief – horror – sadness. He strove to grin; but no, it was true. He was dying; being sucked down into terrifying blackness. Rand had beaten Symes by a flash, a mere flash, by one precious life-saving second.

Jeff Rand was scarcely less shocked than Symes. That dying figure, by all his reckoning, should be his own. Symes shuddered and died.

Good God, did nothing more than a second separate a fellow from eternity? Rand, quaking within, dazedly turned aside and approached his horse, left sheltered between nearby buildings. Giddily he mounted, and for a long while he stood gazing down at the body, round where the sand played and rifted uncaringly. Symes, the fastest man in the south-west, was dead.

Meanwhile, appearing on the street from all directions, came a wild-looking horde of miners, hidden witnesses to that final gunfight. Their worn faces described what suffering they had endured during their long search for the bank-raiding gang; and on passing by Rand, their expressions were of profound awe. They seemed afraid to look at him directly, or to be caught stealing a glimpse at those hands folded on the saddle-horn. Far less dare they take the liberty of uttering one friendly word. To them, it seemed, Rand was a differently formed, dangerous yet superior creature. Such was the heart-rending, friendless and outcasting fame of a gunfighter.

Jeff turned his collar high with one hand, like a person hiding pain; and, wearily flicking the reins, he moved on in silence, plodding steadily down the dead street of Sweetwater.

'Rand! Stop!' called out Mister Sturdy, running across the street and catching hold of the bridle. 'Where are you heading for, Rand?'

Silence answered him; the lonely rider rode on.

'Hopes you ain't sore at my actions, Rand. I'm a US marshal. I've hunted this gang for months. Look here, Jeff. I couldn't prevent Miller's death. I want you to know that. Nor could I stop the killing of Merrick. Smily was my buddy; he was a state man too.' Sturdy paused for breath and began to tug at the bridle. 'Please stop and talk, Rand, won't you?'

The answer was still silence. Rand rode steadily onward, looking directly to the horizon.

'Things should have worked out different to this; I never meant you to get a raw deal.' The grey-headed marshal, beating his thighs with his hat, looked with mournful impatience from side to side. 'When I persuaded you to join us, Rand, I knew you were a clean fighter. I wanted a quick-shooting ally in case my plan went adrift. And it did, when the storm broke up the sheriff's ambush. The sheriff got my message too late to capture the gang in town.' Once again Sturdy started to tug at the bridle. 'Stop, Rand, you must stop!'

Rand kept on riding, appearing to have neither seen nor heard a thing.

'How about your gold?' Mister Sturdy was now flushed and gasping painfully for breath as he floundered through the deeper sand. 'There's a load of your gold back there, it's on the veranda; some more is in Flintstone bank; the remainder is buried in Grapevine Gulch.'

'Give it to Ma Keller.'

It was a husky, emotion-choked reply, yet Sturdy heard it and found his breathlessness suddenly throttling him. Rand halted, and turning he regarded the US marshal's troubled countenance.

'Give me Jim's watch, Bill,' he whispered.

Mister William Sturdy, in a great fluster of eagerness, dived a hand inside a vest pocket, unchained Miller's watch, getting himself unbelievably tangled, and finally handed it up, his smile coming and going uncertainly. Rand took it tenderly, peered at it lengthily, and ultimately concealed it under his coat.

'I'll be taking it out to him,' he murmured simply. 'Goodbye to yuh, Bill.'

'Thanks, Rand, and good luck to you,' Sturdy whispered; he was still striving to maintain a smile as he now released the bridle. 'I'll strike out for the Kellers' place with your gold. Lord, but they'll be mighty pleased! You're saving the old homestead. You're all man, Jeff, all man!'

Rand jerked at the reins and grunted, then broke into a rapid canter, his collar still hiding his expression. Not once did Rand look back. Sometimes there are feelings a man cannot expose, dare not share, but must keep locked up real tight in his soul and speak of them to God.

The lonesome rider, as if heading straight home, drifted towards the sun across the running desert.